HITCHED

HITCHED

Karpov Kinrade

DARING BOOKS

http://KarpovKinrade.com

Copyright © 2014 Karpov Kinrade
Cover Art Copyright © 2014 Karpov Kinrade

ISBN-10: 1939559316
ISBN-13: 9781939559319

Published by Daring Books

Edited by Ally Bishop

You may not use, reproduce or transmit in any manner, any part of this book without written permission, except in the case of brief quotations used in critical articles and reviews, or in accordance with federal Fair Use laws. All rights are reserved.
This eBook is licensed for your personal enjoyment only; it may not be resold or given away to other people. If you would like to share this book with another person, please purchase an additional copy for each recipient. If you're reading this book and did not purchase it, or it was not purchased for your use only, please return to your eBook retailer and purchase your own copy. Thank you for respecting the hard work of this author.

This is a work of fiction. Names, characters, places and incidents are products of the author's imagination, or the author has used them fictitiously.

For Ally Bishop
Because awesomeness

TABLE OF CONTENTS

About Hitched ix
Unexpected Commitment 1
Dr. Sexy..8
What Happens in Vegas 14
From Different Worlds 18
One Summer 29
Bathtub Memories..38
Sweet Music 47
Cigars and Strippers 54
The Remaking of Kacie Michaels 62
Compromises..68
Dinner Dates 72
Blowjobs 77
Home Sweet Home...81
Pool Party for Three 86
Concerns of the Heart..90
Breakfast and Boxers..94
Running..101
A Leap of Faith...106
Getting to Know You..111
Weekend Plans 120
Grey's Anatomy..126
Unexpected Phone Call..133
Blast from the Past 136
Perfect Match 149
The Devil Is in Me, and It's Coming Out.....................154

Dead Poets 157
Meet the Parents..161
Heart to Heart...179
Leap of Faith..184
Bitch Charming..188
Fall Out..191
Moving on...193
Thoughts and Memories..200
Another Heart to Heart...205
Racing with the Stars 209
The Magic Trick..214
Propositions 218
Happily Ever After...223
Déjà Vu..226
No Naughty Deed Goes Unpunished 233
Acknowledgements 239
About Karpov Kinrade...241

ABOUT HITCHED

What happens in Vegas, stays in Vegas…

Or it changes your life forever.

He called me "wife."

This man standing naked in front of me. Tall. Dark. Sexy as sin…

He's my husband?

Disjointed images from the night before, the night I can't entirely remember, float into my mind. Meeting him in the bar. Sharing tidbits of our lives. I own a company that plans bachelor parties. He's a pediatric heart surgeon. We both live in Las Vegas, but we come from very different worlds.

And then I remember that kiss. The way his lips brushed against mine, gentle at first, then harder, deeper, with more urgency. Sex in the elevator. Hot, forbidden, delicious. I remember the way he made me feel. The way our bodies fit perfectly together.

But I don't remember marrying him.

And now, he won't let me go. Dr. Sexy who saves children for a living. He wants the summer to prove we are meant to be.

I can give him a summer.

But can I give him a lifetime?

*This is a contemporary romance novel with a happily ever after. It does NOT have a cliffhanger ending.

ONE

Unexpected Commitment

"Wife?" I look down at the new ring on my left hand and see a similar ring on him as he stalks toward me in all his glorious nakedness. The water from his recent shower gives his ripped, tan body a sexy sheen.

Our bed is disheveled in a way that only all night fucking can accomplish. Empty bottles of Dom Pérignon litter the high-end hotel room I've unexpectedly woken up in. I've retrieved most of my clothes but stand holding one red high heel; the other is still lost somewhere.

"We appear to have had too much to drink last night," he says with a smirk on his handsome face, cobalt blue eyes penetrating. "I think we both got a bit carried away."

I pull my eyes off his body and focus them on his face, which doesn't help me as much as you might think, because this man is the most gorgeous male specimen I've ever seen in my life, and I work with strippers. Well, okay, mostly I work with women since I own a company that plans bachelor and bachelorette parties, and men are more likely to hire strippers than women. But still, I've seen my share, and this man...I can't even...

With all the intelligence of my Ivy League business degree apparently out to lunch, I repeat again, "Wife?"

He's still naked, by the way, as he moves closer to me and reaches for my left hand. Heat floods me as our skin makes contact. He caresses the gold band on my left hand. "Wife."

His voice is husky and deep, and it sends shivers up my spine as my temporary, alcohol-induced amnesia fades, and a memory from the night before makes a belated appearance at the party.

...

I remember him. He was to our right, at a table near the bar, smiling at me with too perfect teeth. My twin brother, Tate, ever the womanizer, nudged me. "I've got my eye on the woman at that table," he said, pointing to a perky blond who was nearly drooling over him. Not that I blamed her. I mean, he's my brother, but I'm not blind. "So you should go for this guy. He's clearly into you."

My best friend, Vi, grinned at me from across the bar, where she'd cozied up to a shy but cute guy that didn't stand a chance against her shapely curves, wild red hair and green eyes. We hadn't been out like this in so long; we'd all been too busy working, building our businesses. Tate works with me at Hitched, and Vi, well...Vi has a unique niche market going in the dominatrix world.

When my brother left me at the bar to woo the panties off the blonde, Mr. Sexy strode over in his suit and tie, exuding confidence, a dark mop of hair offsetting eyes that were an unreal shade of blue. I could tell I was about to have my panties wooed off me as well, and I didn't mind one bit.

"Is this seat taken?" he asked, pointing to where Tate had been sitting.

I smiled. "Not anymore. I think my brother has found someone more exciting to entertain him."

"I find that hard to believe." He slid into the chair, his leg brushing against mine as he pulled in closer.

"Because you know me so well and can with confidence say I'm the most entertaining person here?" I teased, sipping my cocktail.

"I'm good at reading people." He held out his hand, and I took it. "I'm Sebastian Donovan. It's a pleasure to meet you." Instead of shaking my hand, he brought my knuckles to his mouth and, while maintaining eye contact with me, caressed my skin with his lips in a feathery light kiss.

"Kacie Michaels. Nice to meet you," I said as I silently gave my panties notice that they wouldn't be needed for long.

. . .

Other memories are still shadows pulling at my pounding head, trying to break free. "What happened last night?" I ask, still processing the rings. There's no way we tied the knot like drunken assholes in Vegas. Not. Even. Possible.

He hands me some paperwork I hadn't noticed sitting on top of the mahogany dresser. "This happened. I admit to being as surprised as you."

I raise an eyebrow. "I very much doubt that."

His grin falters. "Do you really not remember?"

I look down at the paper. It's a marriage license, signed and stamped and very official looking. Holy shitballs. What the fuck have I done?

"Bits and pieces are coming back," I admit. "But I don't remember this," I say, holding up the paperwork. "This can't be legal."

"I'm afraid it is. I already made a call to my attorney while you were sleeping. Unless you're already married to someone else?" Now he raises his eyebrow, and I scowl.

"I think I'd know if I was previously married."

His lips curve into a sardonic grin, and I sigh at the irony of my own words. "Don't give me that look, dude. This isn't standard operating procedure for me, and I'm guessing—hoping—it's not for you either."

"This is a first," he assures me. "You're the first."

My heart flutters, whether at his words or the way he says them, with heat and desire and all the things that landed me in this spot right now. I know I'm not his first sexual experience. That much is clear. I guess that makes me his first wife. Um, great?

...

As the crowd at the bar grew louder, we moved closer to talk. I couldn't help but notice how good he smelled, a spicy, woody scent with hints of cinnamon and cardamom. It made me want to taste him.

As if reading my mind, mid-sentence he leaned in, cupped my face with his hands, and pressed his lips to mine. He tasted like expensive red wine, and he deepened our kiss, exploring my mouth with his, our tongues teasing each other.

When the kiss ended and he pulled away, I felt deflated and aroused all at once. I missed the feel of him, the contact with his body, and a need grew in me that I hadn't felt in quite some time.

He licked his lips and smiled. "I've been wanting to do that since I first saw you walk in with your brother and friend."

I flushed at the thought that he'd been watching me that long. We'd been here for hours.

"You make quite an impression with a first kiss," I said.

"That's just a taste of what's to come." He winked. I nearly swooned. Not actually swooned, because, you know, I'm not a too-tight-corset-wearing damsel from the Victorian era, but if I'd been standing, there'd for sure be some wobbly knees.

This man. He was delicious, and I wanted more.

I plucked the cherry from my drink and sucked on it in a seductive way. "You're not the only one with skills," I said.

He was sitting so close, his knee was between my legs, one hand on my thigh, pushing up the red dress I was wearing. "Shall we go somewhere and explore these skills in more…depth?"

I didn't need to touch him to tell he had enough in his pants to give true depth to those promises. I reached for my purse and caught Tate's eye. He looked at both of us, then smiled and mouthed, "Have fun!"

We walked out of the bar, Sebastian's hand on my lower back, lingering just a little bit too low, fingers exploring the curve of my ass. And I didn't mind a bit. Believe me, if I did, I'd make my thoughts clear. No one has ever accused me of being too shy to express my feelings.

But right now, with this man, there was only one feeling I wanted to express, and it required considerably less clothing.

...

"We need to get this annulled," I say, my heart racing. "I mean, that shouldn't be hard. I'm guessing this isn't that uncommon in this city."

He holds eye contact with me, and let me just remind you he is *still naked,* and a part of me wants to lick the water off his body and then reenact the parts of last night I'm starting to remember.

"That would probably be the wisest thing to do," he finally says.

I'm relieved. Obviously. Any other feelings that might be surfacing right now, in light of his easy acquiescence, are of no consequence. I push away that flutter of disappointment and straighten my spine. "Of course it is. We barely know each other."

He apparently knows me better than I know him. My memory is coming back, but slowly. I've never been this drunk before. Well, there was one time, back in college, when I got so drunk I almost did a strip tease on a table, but someone had a video camera, and a friend talked me out of it. I didn't remember anything the next day, but that was my first and only drunk black out. Until now.

Marrying a one-night stand definitely beats stripping on film in my book.

TWO

Dr. Sexy

A cell phone rings. Not mine, I realize, looking down at the phone next to me.

Sebastian turns away to reach for his cell charging on the table by the side of the bed. "Doctor Donovan here."

Doctor? While I rack my brain to see if this is information I already had access to, he wraps up the call with monosyllabic responses.

The muscles in his back and shoulders flex, a stress response, perhaps, mirroring the urgency in his voice. He has a tattoo on his back, a stylized image of the moon with stars surrounding it.

I remember that tattoo.

...

We couldn't keep our hands off each other as we walked through the casino toward the elevators. "I have a room here for tonight," he said.

"In anticipation of this?"

"Actually, no. There's a convention here that I was a speaker for. I live in town, but it was easier to get a room. Finding you was a lucky surprise that I intend to take full advantage of."

The elevator binged and opened, and we walked on. I was surprised that no one else crammed in with us, but we didn't waste the privacy.

He pressed me to the wall and ran a hand up my inner thigh, skimming the edges of my panties gently, then pressing harder, spreading my pussy through the satin material and rubbing against my clit. I sucked in a breath and pushed against him as I ran my hand over his cock. It strained against his slacks, desperate to escape.

When he moved my panties to the side and slid a finger, then two, into me, I gasped, wet and ready and needing him so badly that I was nearly choking on desire. "I want you inside me."

"Darling, I want to be inside of you."

Moving so fast I didn't realize what he was doing until he'd done it, he pressed the emergency button and stopped the elevator mid-floor. "I'm going to fuck you hard and fast, but later, I promise I'll take my time," he said as he turned me around, lifted my dress and pulled down my panties. With a knee, he spread my legs more, I heard a rip from a condom wrapper, then felt his cock—hard, huge, urgent—as he thrust himself into me.

Without preamble, without warning, but I didn't care. I was wet and ready, and I pushed my hips against him to take him deeper as he held my waist, fingers digging into me as he did what he'd promised: fucked me hard and fast.

The taboo of it all made me so hot I came just before he did, my body spiraling as muscles clenched and heat pooled in my center, then spread like wildfire.

When he pulled out of me, I braced myself against the wall, adjusted my dress and panties, and he released the emergency button. The elevator started again and opened to his floor, where Vegas vacationers waited for one of the six other elevators positioned around ours.

I was sure everyone was staring, guessing at what we just did, but I didn't care. He held my hand and led me to the executive suite at the end of the hallway. I whistled, impressed. I'd been to company conventions before and never stayed in the penthouse at one of the most expensive hotels on the strip.

The room was everything it should be. Cream furniture with accents of gold and light wood. A balcony overlooked the strip at night, and it took my breath away. By the sliding glass door, a two-person table hosted a basket of fresh fruit and chocolates, and in front of the luxurious cream couch was a matching ottoman with a chilled bottle of champagne and two glasses resting on it.

We skipped all of that and headed straight for the bed.

We undressed each other with more patience than we displayed on the elevator, our most urgent needs temporarily satiated.

I lay back on the bed, spreading my legs as he moved between them, flesh burning at the contact.

He began to fulfill the second half of his promise to me, taking his time to trail kisses from my mouth, down my neck, tracing a line with his tongue over my collarbone and the hollow of my throat. Each touch, each kiss made me quiver in delightful anticipation.

Taking one of my nipples into his mouth, he sucked and nibbled as his hand explored between my legs. I groaned, arching my hips to present my body to him.

Leaving a wet, exposed nipple throbbing, he moved down my belly and held my hips as he dipped his head between my thighs. When his tongue flicked out to tease my labia, I shuddered, reaching for him, my fingers twining in his hair as I pushed him deeper into me.

With skill and patience, he tortured me, circling my clit with his tongue but never touching it.

"More," I moaned, running my fingers through his hair.

"Soon, darling. Remember, I said I'd take my time. And I always mean what I say."

Fuck. This. Man. I needed him to make me come and fuck me. I pulled on his hair, and he licked my pussy from top to bottom in response.

"Why the fuck are you torturing me?" I asked.

He pulled back and grinned. "Because you tortured me all night, darling. I've needed this pussy since I first saw you, but you made me wait. Now it's your turn." And then he continued nipping, sucking, exploring with his mouth and fingers until I was on the edge of a cliff, about to fall into the abyss he'd created.

My fingers fell to his shoulders, digging into his skin as my tightly wound ball of need exploded into shards of color and light. "Oh God, Sebastian. Fuck me!"

Finally, he complied, easing his cock into me, eyes locked on mine as he slowly moved inside of me. His hands explored my body as I gripped him, nails sinking into muscle as our pace increased. When he lifted my legs onto his shoulders to deepen his reach, I cried out in pleasure and adjusted my hips to meet him. With frenetic energy, muscles flexing, he pounded me harder, so hard, so deep, I couldn't breathe or think or do anything accept meet his need with my own, taking him in until I felt as if he'd tear me apart and remake me all at once.

His name was on my lips as I came harder than I could ever remember, and my pussy gripping his cock sent him over the edge too.

After, as he lay on his stomach, head turned to face me, I curled up next to him and traced the tattoos on his back with my fingers. "What do these stars mean?"

He shifted positions and looked up at me. "They represent the battles I lost."

That's all he'd said, and I didn't press further.

Soon thirst and other needs forced us apart.

He smacked my ass playfully as I sauntered to the bathroom. "Hungry, darling?"

I considered. "Sure, I could eat."

And so we dressed and left the hotel room, where the night of drinking commenced.

...

Sebastian hangs up and turns to me. "Darling, I have to go. One of my patients, a six-year-old girl, went into cardiac arrest, and I have to scrub in for surgery."

Oh, God. Fuck me. This guy is too much. Sexy, delicious, and he saves kids for a living? I just can't even.

I suck in my breath. "Of course."

He stalks to me and pulls me into his arms, kissing me deeply as beads of water transfer from his skin to mine. His fingers bury themselves in my deep gold hair, holding my head as the kiss turns full-bodied.

We are both breathless when he pulls away. "I had an amazing night," he says, his eyes holding my gaze. "I hope, as you remember it, that you will feel the same."

He moves away, and my body feels the lack of him and wilts a little. He dresses quickly and then hands me a business card with a phone number scribbled on the back. "Here's my cell. Text me your address, and we'll figure this business out. I've ordered room service, so help yourself and stay as long as you'd like."

Another kiss on the head and he's gone, leaving me alone in the spacious room, still holding my one red shoe.

THREE

What Happens in Vegas

I wander the room, a little lost and a lot hung-over, still looking for my other shoe, which appears to have disappeared entirely. When room service comes, I sign for it and then stare at a table of food meant for two. I don't want to eat, but I know I need something in my stomach to absorb the alcohol.

Copious amounts of carbs, coffee, and orange juice perk me up enough to finish getting ready. I decide a shower sounds nice, since I smell like sex, sweat, and alcohol.

I hate dressing in the clothes I wore all night, but I have no choice. I'm staring down at the marriage license, once again struck dumb by the body double who must have taken over last night, when my phone rings.

"Kacie!" My brother sounds chipper, damn him.

"Hey, Tate. I'll be coming home soon. How was your night?" Better to divert attention away from how my night went.

"Oh, you know, a fun fling I won't ever have to see again."

"Lucky you."

There must be something in my voice, because his tone becomes more serious. "You okay, sis? Did something happen with Mr. Hottie?"

"I'm fine. He was great." So great, I fucking married him. Ha!

He doesn't sound convinced. "Okay, well. I want details. It's about time you got out there and had some meaningless sex with the hottest guy in Vegas, besides me of course."

"Of course," I say with a smile.

"Get your ass home."

"Sure thing."

I hang up and look around once more. His overnight bag is at the foot of the bed, his suit from last night tossed over it. Taking my gold ring off, which is reluctant to leave my finger, I place it next to Sebastian's copy of the marriage certificate. He wanted a text, but that feels like it would open up too much communication between us. Instead, knowing he'd have to come back to get his stuff, I jot down my address and phone number, and leave—without my other shoe.

Exiting the hotel, the heat assaults me, bathing me in a sheen of sweat, choking me with the dry heat, and burning my bare feet with too-hot pavement. Nothing beats Vegas in the summer. I'd leave to spend the season elsewhere if it weren't the biggest moneymaking season of the year.

Tate, Vi and I took a cab here last night, knowing we'd all be too drunk to drive, so I hail one again and get home fifteen minutes later to the welcoming air conditioning of our three bedroom duplex. Tate is wearing a robe and boxer shorts, dark hair artfully messy and blue eyes showing no signs of over-drinking. My eyes, normally the same shade, are blood shot and still hurt.

He hands me a cup of coffee, heavy with the cream and sugar, and raises an eyebrow at my bare feet.

I hold up my shoe. "The other one is MIA," I explain, sipping on the hot and divinely good java.

He appraises me and smiles. "You look like you got good and tumbled last night."

"You have no idea."

"Do tell," he says, gripping my shoulder and guiding me into the living room, where Vi is lounging on the couch, reading a thriller.

"I didn't know you'd be here." I shove her feet off the couch and sit next to her.

"I crashed here last night. Where did you end up?"

I hand her the manila envelope I've been carrying. "Doing this."

Tate looks over her shoulder as she pulls out the paperwork. Her jaw drops. Tate almost spits out his coffee.

"What the actual fuck?" Her eyes are wide. "You married him?"

"Apparently."

Tate pushes me into the middle of the couch and sits next to me. "Honey, we need to have a talk about sex. You don't have to marry the guy just because you fucked him."

I punch his shoulder. "I don't even remember doing it. I drank. A lot."

"No shit." Vi hands me back the license. "What's he like?"

"He's a surgeon who saves the lives of children. So he's pretty much perfect. From what I can recall. He's gorgeous and sexy and amazing in bed. I remember that much. I just don't know how we got from hot sex to 'I do' in the course of a night."

"He must have been some lay," Tate says. "When are you going to see him again?"

"I'm not." But God I want to. This man has ruined sex for me, at least with anyone but him. "This is over. We're getting it annulled. It's the best thing."

"Do you like him?" Vi asks.

"What do you mean?"

She rolls her eyes. "I mean, do you like him? I know you liked the sex. Sounds like the man could seduce a nun and live to tell the tale. Plus, he's a modern day super hero who saves little kids. So, the only other question is, do you like him as a person?"

I think about it a second, but I could have answered right away. "Yes." Even though I don't know him very well, or at least can't remember knowing him, I like him.

She pats my arm, a knowing smile on her lips. "Then, honey, don't blow this. Marriage might have been a bit... extreme on your first night. But that doesn't mean you can't keep dating the man. You don't meet many like him in this world."

FOUR

From Different Worlds

I groan, letting my head flop back against the couch cushion. "My head is going to explode. I'm dying. It's likely a tumor."

Tate scoffs, and Vi jumps up. "Time for my Super Secret Hangover Cure All!"

"Oh God, no! Not that!" I whine. "Anything but that. I thought you were my friend. I thought you loved me."

She darts into the kitchen, ignoring my pleas, and comes out a few minutes later with a glass full of red... something.

"It's tough love. Here you go!"

The first thing you'll notice about Vi's hangover cure is the smell. The fumes alone could kill you. The second is the unnaturally bright red color, like Hollywood blood. But it's the taste that really does you in.

She's never told us the ingredients, but Tate and I made a list once. It included such delicacies as innards of beetles, lava from an active volcano, ash, vomit from a dog that's been poisoned and ate its own shit, and the tears of dying children.

"Drink up. Don't miss a drop, or it won't work."

Hitched

"I hate you."

But I drink. I drink as I feel it eating through my esophagus and trying to claw its way out of me like an alien. I drink as the taste makes me want to cut out my own tongue. I drink until there's nothing left, and I shove the glass back into her hand.

"Never again," I growl, grabbing Tate's water bottle to wash the taste out of my mouth.

"I love you too," she says, sauntering back into the kitchen.

The phone rings, and it doesn't send shooting pain through my brain. The drink is already working. How and why we'll never know. Vi is probably a witch in her spare time.

She comes out to answer it, nods briefly and puts the caller on hold. "It's Joey?"

"He's a regular. Good guy. Lawyer with a lot of friends. He ends up best man to many of them and is always looking for new bachelor party ideas. He got tired of the same old strip clubs, so now he uses us."

She puts him on speaker, and Joey and I exchange pleasantries before he gets to the reason for his call.

"So my buddy's getting married for the third...no, fourth time, and we need to do something really over the top."

I flip through my mental Rolodex and land on something fun and unique. "How about skydiving?"

"That could work. Keep it as a plan B. But I kind of had my heart set on a tank."

"A tank?" I can't keep the surprise out of my voice. Vi rolls her eyes, and Tate looks a bit panicked.

"Yeah, a buddy of mine said he knew a guy who went to Russia and got to ride a tank. You know how to set that up?"

No. We're in Las Vegas, not Russia. Holy fuck. But of course, I don't say that. "I'll look into it." Though in my mind I'm already working on that plan B. "How many guests?"

"Twenty-three."

Tate whistles at the number: it's larger than their usual.

Joey continues. "Kacie, I was wondering, is there any kind of discount for a large party? Because with the divorce, things have been tight, you know?"

Joey told me about his ongoing divorce at our last party. He'd caught his wife sleeping with an old flame from college. Apparently, she'd never stopped loving him. Now, because they didn't have a prenup, they had to split everything down the middle. Joey didn't care too much about that, but they had two kids. He was fighting for them.

"Don't worry. We'll make it work. You'll get the Hitched Frequent Customer Discount." Something I just pulled out of my ass, but whatever.

"Ah, thanks, Kacie. You're a doll."

We hang up, and I go into the kitchen for something to eat while Tate starts typing on his laptop. "Kacie, there's no way in hell we're going to get a tank for these guys, you know that right?"

"I know." I find some cheese and crackers. Good enough.

"So what's the plan?" he asks, still googling the impossible.

"The plan is to create an adventure that will make him forget about tanks and Russia and remember why he loves us and Las Vegas so much."

Vi heads to the kitchen for coffee. "You're too good to these people. I could never do your job."

"I'm pretty sure I could never do yours either," I say, thinking about what it must be like to work as a Dominatrix. "Oh, I nearly forgot!" I leave the food on the counter and run to the closet by our front door to pull out a bag. "I bought stuff for my super stealthy plan to put Hitched on the celebrity map!"

Tate rolls his eyes. "This is so lame, Kacie. The cheese factor is at stench level."

I stick my tongue out at him. "You're just jealous you didn't think of it first."

I dump everything onto the coffee table and start assembling my masterpiece.

Vi comes back in and sits next to me. "What's this?"

"It's Kacie's latest 'business plan,'" Tate says, using air quotes.

"Shut up, Tate. Until you come up with something better, we're doing this." I turn to Vi to explain as I hold up a toy car. "You heard the news that David Melton's getting married, right?"

Her eyes light up. "Melton, as in the famous magician who performs at the Wynn? The guy who literally disappeared, without any props, live in front of thousands of people?"

"That's the one!"

"He's getting married? That bastard! He's *my* magical goth-rock-star-celebrity husband. He just doesn't know it yet," Vi says, fanning herself dramatically.

"You'll have to fight his fiancée for him."

"I'm a patient woman. I can wait for the divorce."

I laugh. "And such a romantic. Anyways, I want Hitched to land his bachelor party. So...I'm sending him a basket with little gifts that represent my ideas for his party, along with a handwritten note pitching him my idea. I did some research, and he's a huge fan of Michael Schwartz, the racecar driver, and loves race cars. So I'm including miniature high-end cars, a helicopter, handcuffs, champagne, whipped cream and a few other trinkets. The plan is to host his party on the roof of the Wynn and have a helicopter pick him and a few of his closest friends up to take them to the tracks to race. What I'm really hoping is that I can get Schwartz himself to show up. But I'm not promising that yet, since it's not a done deal."

I add the finishing touches to the basket, and then I tuck my card, our brochure, and the letter I wrote inside and wrap it up. "Voila!"

Vi examines the basket. "I like it. I think it's clever and fun and unique. I have a good feeling about this."

I flip Tate off and smile. "See? This is going to work. Melton will be blown away, he'll book us, we'll rock his world, and he'll tell all his celebrity friends about us. It's going to launch us onto the next rung of the business ladder," I insist.

"Want me to deliver it? I'll be driving by the Wynn today, and I know some people there who can help make sure it gets to him," Vi says, standing and grabbing her purse.

"Oh, that would be great. Thank you!" I hand her the basket and kiss her cheek. "You're the best."

She tosses her hair over her shoulder. "I know. But it's good to be reminded."

As Vi heads out, she runs into a deliveryman coming up the stairs. "Someone's got a package," Vi hollers as she walks away. "I wonder who it could be from."

Don't judge me for the butterflies I get in my stomach. You know you'd get them too if there was any possibility that the hot guy you spent the night with had just sent you something. Not that he has. I'm sure it's just...a mistake or wrong address or something.

When I get to the door, a man is standing there with a long white box wrapped in thick red ribbon. "Miss Michaels?"

"That's me."

He holds out the box. "This is for you." When I take the box, he holds out a clipboard. "If you could just sign here." He points to a line, and I scribble my signature and close the door.

I carry it into the living room and sink onto the red couch I talked Tate into letting me buy for our house. The ribbon on the box slips off easily, and when I open the box, I find two dozen long stemmed red roses, my missing red shoe and a card.

My hand is trembling as I tear through the thick parchment envelope. When I open it, a gold ring falls out. My wedding ring. The note is written in neat cursive.

My darling Kacie,

I know our relationship started unexpectedly and proceeded with too little caution, but I can't get you out of my mind. Like Cinderella, you lost your shoe, and I endeavor to make mine the only woman who should be wearing it. Watch for another package tomorrow, and please keep tomorrow evening free. I'll pick you up at seven o'clock, and we can discuss our future, for there will undoubtedly be one if I have anything to say about it.

Yours truly and always,
Sebastian

Tate, the busybody that he is, snatches the note from me and reads it aloud. "That's so sweet," he says, his voice too syrupy. "You should definitely see him again. And fuck him again. He sounds perfect. If I were gay—and he were gay, obviously—I'd totally go for it."

I grab the note back from him. "If you were gay, you'd bang him one night and never call him again. I don't think being gay would change your genetic makeup of love 'em and leave 'em."

He grins like an idiot. "But what a night it would be."

"Go away now, please. I will go, but only to discuss the annulment. Nothing more."

He wags his eyebrows. "That's what they all say. Until it's cock-o-clock."

"Gross. You didn't seriously just say that did you? That better not become a thing. I don't ever want to hear that spoken aloud again."

I take my package up to my room and think about the note.

I should be irritated that Sebastian would be so presumptuous about my evening plans and entire future, but my stomach dances with those butterflies. I want to see him again. Need to see him again.

My pigheaded stubbornness does its best to present all the reasons why getting involved with this guy is a very bad idea. We met in a drunken haze of sex and need, and that's no way to start a healthy relationship. I barely know him. I don't want anything serious right now. I like to keep my life simple, orderly, focused.

The list is endless, but underneath all of that, my heart is adamant that I must see him again. Must kiss him and feel his lips against mine. Must taste him.

Must have him.

With this in mind, I slip the ring through my silver necklace and tuck it beneath my shirt, just so I can give it back to him without losing it. I'm grateful he sent back my shoe, and I place it with its twin, then put the roses in a vase and center it on my dresser. No point in wasting beautiful flowers.

As for the note, I stick it in my red Coach bag and try to forget about it for now.

I reach for my MacBook and fire it up, doing a search for annulments in Las Vegas. Turns out, it's not that hard, especially if both parties agree. Assuming the judge rules that I was in fact incapable of making informed consent given my state that night.

I print out the forms we need, sign and fill out what I can, and stick them in my purse next to his note. Even *if* we end up fucking again—the thought of him inside me makes me wet—once we get these signed and notarized, we'll be set. It shouldn't take more than a few weeks for the annulment to be final and our lives to go back to normal.

Now I feel better. Mostly better. Definitely better. Maybe in a few years when our business is booming, and we can move into bigger events and party planning, when I can hire a bigger staff and step away from the day-to-day operations a little more, maybe then the timing will be better for me to think about something serious.

I go downstairs to rejoin my brother and figure out a way to get Joey off his "tank" kick.

"Hey, sis." Tate says, feet resting on the coffee table as he works on his laptop. "Come to any major life decisions up there all alone in your room?"

"Everything is sorted out. I'll be seeing him tomorrow to finalize things." My heart does a little skip at that, but I ignore the traitorous beast.

Tate doesn't look convinced. He raises an eyebrow, his blue eyes reading too much into my face, I'm sure. Damn him for knowing me so well.

I sigh with more drama than the situation requires and flop onto the couch next to him. "Stop looking at me like that. Yes, he was the most amazing sex I've ever had. And yes, he's an amazing catch in a sea of slimy serpents, but he's not for me. We're from two different worlds. It would never work. What could a girl with a business degree who plans bachelor parties possibly have in common with a fucking pediatric heart surgeon?"

He throws his arm over my shoulder. "I don't know. But there's no harm in finding out, right?"

...

I'd like to say that I hadn't given any thought to the package Sebastian promised would be arriving today. I'd like to say that over the last twenty-four hours my mind never drifted to the few memories I still have of our tumultuous night together. That I didn't scamper to the front door like a dog every time I heard something that could possibly be construed as a delivery.

I'd like to say all of those things. But you and I both know that would be a load of a shit, right?

I know I'm not the first woman to feel these flutters of butterflies at the mere thought of a man, but I still feel like a numskull, nonetheless. This isn't me. This has never been me. While my high school girlfriends were going crazy about boys, I was studying. While my college friends were crushing on guys, I was having meaningless flings to satiate needs while I stayed focused on my life plans.

Running a business like mine might not seem like the loftiest of goals, but it was a strategic plan on my part to build something small into something big. This is a market in demand, regardless of the economy. People want their wedding, and their pre-wedding parties, to be memorable. And people, men in particular, like their strippers. And I like running my own life, having a career that I control, not working for someone else who tells me when I can eat and use the bathroom and make a phone call. I'm too autonomous for that shit. So this business suits me perfectly. And I have big plans for expansion.

Men, relationships, emotional attachments—those just complicate shit. It makes the whole world muddled. I've seen it happen to my girlfriends time and again, women I hardly ever see anymore. Women who don't have time for the things they loved before.

I don't want to be one of those women.

That's why I'm not going to let Dr. Sexy woo me beyond one night.

So when the doorbell rings (finally, fuck!) and I accept the package I know is from him, I refuse to acknowledge the schoolgirl giddiness I'm feeling in the pit of my stomach.

But Tate watches me pull off the red ribbon from the box with his knowing grin, and I want to smack it off of him.

"Fuck off," I tell him as I open the lid.

"You're all talk, my love-sick twin."

With all the maturity born of years of study, I stick my tongue out at him and then suck in my breath when I see what's in the box. With shaking hands I pull out the most stunning red dress, shoes and matching lipstick. Russian Red, the Mac label says. But I'm more focused on the clothes. A pair of designer shoes, and a dress that I know put him out a shit ton of money. (That's a real amount by the way. You can look it up. It'll have a picture of this dress and these shoes next to it.)

Tate whistles. "This is what he sends you for your breakup dinner?"

"It's not a break up dinner. We were never together. Not really." But my voice lacks conviction because I'm now reading the note, and maybe there's a tear in my eye, but I refuse to admit that.

I tuck the card away, and Tate waits.

"I'm not sharing that part. It's personal."

"Too personal for me? It must be huge, then," he says.

And it is. It's huge because it's so simple. So tender. So unexpectedly pure. And I can't think about it or look at it or read it because it destroys my resolve, and tonight I will need all my resolve to finish this once and for all.

FIVE

One Summer

The rest of the day is wasted. We try to work; we get a few plans down for marketing and ideas for this summer season of parties. Business will take off soon. It always does this time of year, especially in Vegas, and we want to be ready to take on all of the clients we know will be coming our way.

I put off dressing for my non-date until the latest possible moment, my mind and body at war with what they want from the night.

The dress fits perfectly, hugging all my curves as if it had been made for my body alone. The shoes give height to my short frame, and I fall in love with them the moment I put them on. Damn that man.

When the doorbell rings, I know it's not a delivery, but the man himself, and I experience a case of serious nerves. I'm not the wilting flower type, if you hadn't guessed that by now. I can hold my own in most any situation, but right now I'm about to melt out of my dress, and I haven't even seen him yet.

I can hear Tate opening the door and letting him in, and I hurry to swipe my lips with Russian Red lipstick, grab my purse—which has all the important documents in it—and act like I'm not a basket of butterflies as I walk—gracefully, I like to imagine—down the stairs.

Tate is talking to him, and they are laughing, and I want to smack my brother and tell him not to bond with the man I won't likely see again after today.

Sebastian looks up and stops talking; instead his eyes eat me up, and he smiles this small, secret smile that makes me think naughty thoughts about what that mouth is capable of achieving between my legs. Instead of my usual witty retort, I pause. Struck by him. He's wearing a suit and tie, very high end, tailored to his muscular, tall body, his dark hair just a bit ruffled, like he recently ran his hands through it.

I remember his hair, thick under my palm, as I held his head while he licked me and made me come.

Argh! I want to scream from frustration, but instead I smile. "Hello, Sebastian."

He holds out a hand as I reach the last stair. "Ms. Michaels, you look stunning."

"Thank you for the dress and shoes," I say.

His eyes darken. "It's not the dress, or the shoes, that make you stunning, darling."

Breathe. Just. Breathe.

"You have a way with words, Dr. Donovan. A better bedside manner than most in your profession, I imagine."

Tate clears his throat. "I'll leave you two to your evening." He kisses me on the cheek and retreats upstairs to his own room, but not before turning and giving me a meaningful look. "Remember what I said, Kacie."

I scowl at him before turning back to my non-date. "Shall we go?"

...

I won't bore you with recounting the drive to the restaurant. Expensive car. Small talk. Hands brushing against each other once or twice. Blah, blah, blah.

I will say that by the time we arrived at the restaurant, my panties were expecting something hot because they were wet. Damn. That. Man.

Even in the evening, Las Vegas's summers are scorching. It never cools off—just gets a bit darker. Fortunately, we only have to walk a few steps in the sweltering heat before the blast of air conditioning from the restaurant dries the sweat on my skin. Once we're escorted to our table, I sit and sip at the water immediately placed in front of me, grateful for something cold to drink.

Sebastian stares at me like I'm his dinner, and he hasn't eaten in days.

"You're making me nervous," I say, though that's only partially true. I can handle myself well enough, but something about him, about the way he looks at me, throws me off balance.

"I don't mean to. I just find you mesmerizing." He smiles. "Have you had any luck remembering more of our night together?"

"Some. The actual marriage part is still a haze, but I do remember meeting you and...other things."

"I want you to know, I wouldn't have married you if I'd known you were too drunk to consent. I would never take advantage of you that way. But I don't regret it either."

His voice is intoxicating, but I need to change the subject before this goes too far. "I remember the tattoo, on your back. Of the stars. You said it was of battles lost. What did you mean?"

His face turns serious. "I'm an excellent surgeon. I'm not bragging; I've worked hard to become one of the best. But I'm not God. Sometimes…sometimes I can't save a child. When that happens, when someone dies on my table or in my care, I add a star to the tattoo. I need them to know they will never be forgotten. Not by me."

I can't remember how many stars he had on his back. Not too many, but enough. Each the life of a child he couldn't save. "What made you decide to become a pediatric heart surgeon?"

"My little sister was born with a bad heart. I wanted to fix her so badly, but as a child myself, I was helpless. The doctors at the hospital I now work at saved her life. My mentor, actually, was her surgeon. I knew then I wanted to do what he did. Now, it's my goal to put Sunrise Children's Hospital on the map as the leading hospital for pediatric care."

"Wow, that's quite a goal."

He smiles. "What about you? What are your life goals?"

"Nothing that impressive. I want Hitched to become the go-to party planner for celebrity clients. I want to grow big enough to franchise and create something truly lasting. I know it sounds shallow and silly compared to your life."

He reaches over the table and places his hand over mine. "You bring joy to people during the most memorable time in their lives. Your goals and dreams are just as important as mine. And I respect a woman who has ambition and knows what she wants in life."

His response surprises me. "Really?"

"Really. You have my respect Ms. Michaels. We are meant to be in each other's lives. I believe that."

With those words, he tugs at my heart in ways I don't expect. Too overcome with emotion to carry on our conversation, I excuse myself to use the restroom. I feel flustered, and I need to compose myself so we can discuss the business at hand: the end of our very brief marriage.

I'm alone in the posh bathroom, reapplying my red lipstick, when I hear the door open, then close with a click.

I expect another woman coming in to freshen up and am shocked when Sebastian is there in the reflection of the mirror.

"This is the ladies room," I say.

"I know." His voice is husky.

I put my lipstick away and turn to face him. "Someone could come in at any moment."

This does not get the desired reaction. He moves closer, hands gripping my hips as he gazes at me with a hungry look in his eyes.

"I locked the door. We have a few moments."

"For what?" Now my voice is thick with desire.

"For this." He lifts me onto the counter with an easy move, hiking up my dress to the very top of my thighs as he spreads my legs and claims my lips with his.

I'm breathless, needy, and in that moment, I don't give a flying fuck who might walk in or what people might say or why we're actually on this non-date to begin with. All I want is him. Inside me. Now.

His fingers move aside the satin cloth of my panties and slip into my wet and throbbing pussy. "I've wanted you since I left the hotel yesterday morning."

Has it only been since yesterday? It seems like so much longer.

"When I saw you in this dress, in this lipstick, all I wanted to do was take it off you. I planned to wait until later, but I can't wait. Fuck me, Kacie. Fuck me now."

I spread my legs wider and push my hips forward. He pulls his fingers out of me, and for a moment I feel empty, but then he unzips his pants, puts a condom on, and shoves his hard cock into me, deep and thick, filling me to the point of almost pain.

"Fuck," I say, smiling. "You feel even better than I remembered." And it's true; he does. My memories don't compare to the glorious man inside me.

His grin turns playful. "Then just wait until I make you come."

"Oh, God yes." I desperately want to come on his cock.

With his hands on my hips, my arms around his shoulders, we move together as we strain to become one, to get closer, to take more of each other and give more of ourselves.

When he's close to coming, he slips a hand between us and uses his thumb to rub my clit, sending pulses of pleasure through my body, sensations overlapping as he rubs and fucks and moves inside of me and on me, and when I come it's hard, fast, sharp and followed immediately by his own orgasm.

I rest my forehead on his chest and catch my breath.

"I could get used to this," he says.

I look up at him and grin. "Don't you want to know if I'm satisfied?" I ask. "If my orgasm was better than last time?"

"I know it was," he says. Cocky bastard.

Then he kisses me again, caressing my face, trailing kisses up my chin until he lands on my lips. "You are a delicious woman," he says, his breath moving on my skin, sending a shiver of desire through my body.

Someone knocks on the door, and he pulls out. We both clean up as quickly as we can and walk out as two women ogle us. I can't help but giggle. "They must be thinking the worst of us," I say.

Sebastian puts an arm around my waist and tucks me against him. "I care not at all what other people think of me, Kacie. As long as you enjoyed it."

"I did," I admit. He holds my chair as I sit, and once he's sitting across from me, I pull out my purse. Wine has already been served in my absence, and I take a sip and think about what I want to say next.

"I brought the papers we need to fill out and sign. Within a few weeks, this will all be behind us."

I hand the neat stack of legalese to him, and he studies each page methodically as I sip my wine and try to keep my hands steady. His eyes are a dark blue—that cobalt blue that first attracted me to him when he came to introduce himself at the bar, and I wish for a moment that he was looking at me and not the stupid papers.

To keep myself busy, I pull a pen out of my purse and push it his way. "There were things I couldn't fill out about you."

He nods, continues to read, and when the server brings us fresh bread with garlic butter, I use the food as the distraction I need to survive such a long silence.

The bread is so good I nearly die of carb addiction right then and there. I eat three pieces before he finally puts the paperwork down and reaches for my hand, which—oh God—has a bit of butter on it.

He sees the butter and the utter horror in my eyes, and instead of just letting go so I can wipe my own hand, he...

Damn. That. Man.

He sticks my fingers in his mouth and sucks. Slowly. Deliciously. And I want to drag him back to the bathroom for round two because I can still feel the ache that having him inside me created, and the other kind of ache that having him pull out of me left.

But instead, I gently withdraw my hand, wipe it on a cloth napkin and glance at the pen. "It would be easier if we can just get the paperwork out of the way now. I'm happy to drop this off and file it all, no problem. I know you must be a very busy man."

He nods. "I am. So busy I've deprived myself of a lot of things to become who I am. And now I find that those things I thought were trivial, incidental, not relevant to the meaningful life I'm creating...some of them have turned out to be the most important. Love, family, connection. Bearing witness to another's journey and knowing she bears witness to mine...that we will grow and share the most precious of our moments on earth with each other. I thought I didn't need any of that to be happy."

He reaches for my hand again and strokes the inside of my wrist with his thumb, softly, gently. "I was wrong," he says, his eyes so deep I want to swim in them.

I don't know what to say because I'm not sure what he's trying to say. Or maybe I do know what he's trying to say, but I don't want to know. I want to stick to the plan. I like plans. They have gotten me through life well. I don't like this off-the-book nonsense.

He stacks the paperwork back into its neat pile, which I appreciate, and pushes it back to me, unsigned. Which I most definitely do not appreciate.

"Kacie, I don't know what it is about you, but I can't let you go. I want to know you better. I want you to know me better. Give me this summer. One summer to show you we're meant to be together. If at the end of the summer you don't want what we have, I'll sign your papers. But by the end of the summer, you won't want me to."

SIX

Bathtub Memories

I freeze, stunned, unsure how to respond. Of course I can't stay married to him all summer long. That's absurd. Ridiculous. Totally outrageous.

"No! You have to sign these. We have to end this now. It's not right. We're not right. We don't belong together."

He smiles, and I melt a little, but I refuse to let him see that.

"We do. I think somewhere inside that pragmatic mind of yours, you know that. But it's okay; we have time for me to show you how right we are for each other, and how wrong you are to think otherwise."

I'm getting angry for real now. "You can't force me to date you." I stand, grabbing my paperwork. "I'll hire a lawyer and make this happen without your signature."

He nods and light from the candle on the table reflects in his eyes. "You could do that, at considerable expense, and without my signature, it would still take all summer to finalize. I promise you my way will be much less expensive and more pleasurable."

I grab my purse and give him a glare I hope sets him on fire. "This is over. We are over. I'm not interested in your outlandish proposal."

It feels good to stomp away from him in all my fire and brimstone anger. Until I get outside and realize I have no way home.

Sheepishly, I call Tate, who doesn't answer. I call Vi, and she answers on the first ring. "Kacie, what's up babe? Did you marry another total stranger today?"

"Hardy, har, har, bitch. No, I'm trying to annul the one I'm already married to, but he's not signing the fucking paperwork. I just walked out on our non-date discussion, and I was hoping you could pick me up?" I give her the address.

"Sure, I just finished up with a client. Let me change into normal people clothes, and I'll be right over."

Her normal people clothes include spiked nails with silver tips over ruby red polish. A red fedora and black leather pants with red high heels and a corset with red and black roses. We don't share the same idea of "normal," but I still love her, and right now, I love her a ton. I hug her after sliding into the passenger side of the car.

"Haven't you learned to always drive to a date in your own car?" she asks as she pulls out.

"It was tricky." I explain what happened.

"That doesn't sound tricky, that sounds hot. Why are you ditching this guy for a night at home with just your brother and best friend for company?"

"Shut up. You would not find this hot if it was happening to you. This alpha male 'I'm taking charge of this relationship, and I know what's best' bullshit. I'm not a cave woman to be knocked on her head and dragged back into the cave for a good fuck." But even as I say the words, warmth fills me at the thought of him pulling me into a cave—not by the hair, mind you, but, I don't know, with some ferocity—and fucking me hard by the light of a fire with the cold night air cooling our skin.

"Earth to Kacie, we're home." She stops the car, and I realize I probably missed something she said in my sex-hazed daydreaming.

"Thanks for the ride, Vi. You coming in?"

She shrugs. "Sure. But only if you have liquor. This feels like a night to drink our worries away."

I laugh. "I think I've already drank too much away, don't you? But I'll have one glass of wine."

I'm sure it will surprise no one to discover that by the time midnight strikes, we've finished off two bottles between the three of us. Vi is staying the night in our guest room, and I'm not sure I'm leaving the couch. Tate tosses me a bottle of water, which falls to the ground beside me.

"Drink up, sis, or you'll feel like shit tomorrow."

"That seems inevitable either way," I say, as my high starts to leave me with a hint of headache coming in to replace it.

"Not if you hydrate and take some ibuprofen. And eat an orange." He smiles wickedly and walks into the kitchen to get all the prescribed ingredients.

"You sound like our mother," I accuse him.

"No, she would tell you to stop drinking; it's not ladylike."

I laugh, but it comes out like a very unladylike snort. "True. She would. We should call them. I'm sure they miss us and are just too polite to call because they always think they're bothering us."

He returns with two pink pills and slices of oranges. "They *are* usually bothering us. And you must be really drunk if you think you want to talk to our parents."

I take the pills, eat an orange slice and drink as much water as I can without vomiting. "Be nice. Didn't anyone ever teach you to respect your elders?"

He slouches in the overstuffed chair to my side and grins. "I respect one thing, sis. Okay, two things. Money and sexy women."

I reach for a throw pillow, and, well, I throw it at him. It hits him square in the face, and he reacts as if I just beat him with a cast iron skillet. "If I really believed you were that shallow, we would not be business partners," I say.

"Speaking of…" He stands and walks to our answering machine. Shut up, yes, we still have one of those, just for business. It makes it easier for both of us to check messages and to screen calls when we're off duty. Don't mock.

He hits play, and it's a guy's voice who introduces himself as Dan. "I need you to plan a bachelor party for my brother in two weeks. You come highly recommended from a friend."

"Woohoo!" I scream. "We're getting referrals; this is awesome."

Tate grins from ear to ear. "Yup! It's starting to happen. Everything we dreamed about."

"Well, one referral is hardly everything, but I'll take it." I pull out my iPad and make some notes, write down Dan's phone number and then block out the date for his party. "I'll give him a call tomorrow to set things up and find out what he wants, then I'll book the girls for that night. Will you handle the alcohol order and secure a bartender?"

He rolls his eyes. "I didn't play this for you to freak out and start working at one in the morning. While drunk. I just wanted you to know we had a job coming up. Relax, we'll start working tomorrow."

...

And we do. I don't let a little hangover stop either of us from setting up this new job. Dan is more than happy to book everything we can offer, from the music to the strippers to the open bar. I take a lot of notes during our call and thank him for choosing us, then type up everything for Tate and I to divide and conquer.

"There will be about fifteen guys in attendance, and he wants the booze to flow freely. He's sending the deposit via PayPal today. Once we have it, we can book everyone. He said he already has a room reserved for it at the Bellagio, so we're all set on that end."

We get three more parties booked today, and none of them overlap each other, which is a miracle that makes me smile. I'm almost able to push Dr. Sexy out of my mind. Almost.

When the doorbell rings, I don't even wonder about it, until I see the delivery person with another gift box and a vase full of jasmine and white lilies. I sign, and the guy smirks at me in a knowing way. I resist the urge to slap the smirk off his face.

Inside the box is a golden silk bag with a miniature golden bathtub filled with bath products. Salts, lotion, bath soap and bath oils. I can't bear to throw the flowers away, so I put them on our kitchen table next to the others, but I toss the bath set in the trash, unwilling to indulge these gifts any longer.

He can't force me to stay married to him, the asshat. Married life, kids, the whole picket fence thing—it's fine for some, for many even, and someday it'll probably be something I want. But not today. Not now.

The doorbell rings again, but then the door opens, and Vi walks in, her high heels clicking against the hardwood floors in our entryway. "Good evening, kids. It's time to play!"

I hug her and holler for Tate. "Are you two going out?" It's not unusual for the two of them to go out if I'm not up for it. We met Vi when we first moved here just over a year ago, and the three of us became instant BFFs. We wouldn't have survived the first six months in Las Vegas without her.

"The three of us are going out. You need to either fuck the sexy doctor, or fuck someone else to put him out of your mind."

I hate that she knows me so well. "I can't go out tonight. Too much work to do. But you and Tate have fun."

Tate lumbers down the stairway taking three stairs at a time and looking like a million bucks. Vi whistles. "Looking good, Mr. Michaels. Some girl is about to lose her heart tonight. Poor thing."

Tate scowls at me. "You should come. All work and no play..."

"Yeah, that served me so well last time," I joke.

He shrugs, knowing when to pick his battles. "Fine. We're off. Call if you want to join."

They each kiss me on the cheek, and when they leave, the house is suddenly very quiet and lonely.

I spend a few hours pretending to work, mostly making notes and lists and daydreaming about things I shouldn't.

I finally give up the pretense and decide to take a bath. My eyes wander to the trash bin with the lovely bath set. No one would know if I used it, just a little. Right? Casting my eyes about as if someone might be spying on me and reporting back to Dr. Sexy that yes, I did indeed partake of his gifts, as if this is somehow consent to staying married, I grab the bath kit and head upstairs.

Tate and I have lived together all of our lives, even through college and grad school, so I don't often get time alone. I treasure it, and tonight I set the mood with soft music, candles, a glass of red wine and a salted bubble bath with extra hot water.

As I sink into the luxurious heat, my body breathes a sigh of relief. The tension and stress from the last few days drains out of me, and I close my eyes and lean back, enjoying the music, the sips of wine, the calm.

But it doesn't take long for my mysterious future ex-husband to creep into my mind, undoing my reverie with memories of our torrid night together.

His hotel room had an extra large bath, one we used to full avail.

He undressed me slowly, his long fingers and strong hands caressing my body with each movement as I stood still, breathing deeply, taking in the moment. I stood naked before him while he was still fully clothed, and the disparity between us sent waves of erotic charge through me.

As I pull this memory up and view it like a movie in my mind, my hand dips under the soapy water and between my legs. I spread my labia and tease my clit, slipping a finger inside of me as I remember him doing the same that night.

His hand over my mound, finger exploring my wet center, my pussy aching for more of him. I could see his cock through his slacks, hard and demanding, and I wanted to free him from that constraint, but I also wanted to continue enjoying this moment as he worshiped me with his eyes and explored me with his body.

I rub at my clit, fingering myself as I use my other hand to tease my nipples. I want this to be him touching me, his fingers, his hands, his tongue and mouth. His cock. But I settle for the memories as I bring myself closer to climax.

He knelt in front of me, his mouth positioned at my pussy as he flicked a tongue out and lightly licked my clit. My body shuddered, knees weak as he pushed his tongue deeper into me, fingers digging into my hips, holding me tightly against his mouth. My hands fell to the top of his head, to his thick dark hair as he pleasured me beyond reason. The bath filled with water as I came hard in his mouth. He finally let me undress him, just before lifting me up and placing me in the steaming bath. He got in beside me, then pulled me onto his lap, impaling me on his hard cock.

My wet pussy took him in greedily, eagerly, and our bodies rocked together in the water, his hands exploring my breasts, waist, hips, his fingers finding my sensitive, swollen clit and sending me over the edge again, quickly this time, as I came on his cock.

I'm nearly there, the memory of him inside me tipping the scale as I come to thoughts of him, alone in my bathtub.

And I realize then that getting him out of my mind is not going to be as easy as signing a few papers.

SEVEN

Sweet Music

Every day for the last week Sebastian has sent me flowers and a gift, delivered to my house. I'm setting up another dozen roses in a vase when Tate walks in from his morning run.

"You need to call the guy back, sis. It's starting to look like a funeral in here."

"I'm not giving in just because he's burying me in a flower garden. I refuse to be coerced into marriage, even to him."

Tate raises an eyebrow. "At least you're acknowledging that he's different. That's a start."

I huff, not wanting to talk about this any more. "Are we all set with the liquor for tonight?"

Tate nods. "But I got a call while running. The bartender we hired called in sick."

I frown. "Seriously? The day of our bachelor party? That sucks. I'll call Vi and see if she can cover."

I can tell Vi is still sleeping when she answers. "Sorry to wake you," I say. "But I need a favor."

I give her the details, and she agrees to fill in. "I had a date with Chad, that guy I met the night you got hitched..."

"Funny."

"Anyways, can I bring him? I promise we won't get in the way."

"Sure, no problem. He can help Tate as a bouncer if we need it."

She laughs. "Probably not; he's more the submissive type. But he can help me serve drinks. He was a bartender in college."

Of course Vi would go for the guy she could more easily control. "That sounds fine. Thanks so much." I give her the address and time. "So, things are going well with Chad? You usually don't date one-night-stands."

"He's sleeping next to me right now. We were up all night." And then, as if I didn't quite understand her meaning, she added, "fucking."

"Yeah, I got that, but thanks. I'm glad. I look forward to meeting him."

I assume I didn't meet him that night. He and Vi were already gone by the time I got really drunk.

"Okay, great. See you then, Kacie."

Two hours before the party, Nicole and Jasmine arrive to go over the itinerary. They're the best exotic dancers we work with, and I'm glad they were both available for tonight. Especially since this was a referral.

I hug them each, and Tate kisses them both on the cheek. Neither is dressed provocatively. Nicole is tall with long natural blond hair, blue eyed, full breasts, a thin waist and legs a mile long, but she's wearing normal jeans and a t-shirt with a large black bag thrown over her shoulder. Likely her costume for tonight.

Jasmine is her opposite: petite, honey-skinned with silky black hair that's cropped just under her ears in a stylish bob. She has a five-year-old daughter at home and is in school to become a paralegal. Nicole was a professional ballerina until an injury took her out of the game. Men at our parties only know them as sex objects to be lusted after, but I know the real women behind the persona. I used to feel badly for them, but I can tell they really enjoy their jobs, and they are well paid, so I've made my peace with it. As long as they don't feel exploited or forced into anything, then it works.

And at Hitched, we don't do sex. While it might be legal in some parts of Nevada, it's not legal in Las Vegas, and it's not the kind of business Tate and I want to run regardless. We decided early on that we want to run a high-end bachelor party business that caters to specialty clients in a classy and fun way.

Without the "extras" other companies sometimes provide, legal or not.

...

"You ladies ready for tonight?" I ask as I straighten my short black skirt and red sleeveless blouse. I'm going for professional but sexy. It's a tough balance, but I think this outfit strikes the right chord.

Nicole grins. "Sure. This is a pretty small party. I think we can handle them."

I glance at Jasmine, who's putting on a coat of lipstick. "How's your daughter?"

Jasmine smacks her cherry red lips and smiles. "Great. She's so excited for kindergarten this fall she won't stop talking about it. I can't get any peace, but I love it."

"Is the dad still being an asshole with child support?" Tate asks. He can't stand deadbeat dads and would beat the shit out of all of them if he could, not that I blame him.

Jasmine rolls her eyes. "Yes, but thankfully we're doing okay. Working for you is really helping. Your clients are the best tippers."

I beam at that, pleased that our business gives her some perks over working for someone else.

My heart flutters as we leave the house. I check my phone, hoping I got a message from a certain famous magician. Nothing. I don't let it get me down. I know we'll get the job, but tonight, I have a client to focus on. I still get nervous right before a party, but once it gets rolling, the butterflies settle, and I'm flying high.

I take my own car, and Tate takes his. The women join Tate. They like to tease him, and I enjoy watching him blush under their friendly flirtations.

We arrive at the hotel room before anyone, which is good. I want to be set up before the groom and his friends get here. My name is on the reservation, and Tate gives all of our bags full of party supplies to the bellhop to take up.

The room is perfect. I worry when someone else books the space whether it will be a tight room with the bed monopolizing the area we need to work, but this is a suite with a spacious living area, a bar and a balcony overlooking the Strip. The bedroom is separate and will be a good place to keep our gear while the guests enjoy the celebrations in the main room.

Hitched

Vi arrives shortly after us, dressed in her standard leather and lace. Chad, a slim-framed man with beautiful green eyes and short brown hair is at her side and casts adoring gazes at her frequently. He's definitely smitten.

"Thank you for filling in," I tell her.

"No problem." She introduces Chad to the four of us, and I shake his hand. "It's nice to meet you."

"You too," he says, his smile bringing out a dimple in his cheek. He looks around the room, still grinning. "This is nice. Thanks for letting me come and help." He holds up a guitar case and looks sheepishly at me. "I know this is probably not the right venue, but I play and sing if you need a change of music tonight. No pressure."

I raise a brow in surprise, and Vi laughs at my expression. "He's quite amazing. I promise."

I can't let him audition with a live audience, so I guess I have to listen to him now. If you've ever been in a situation where you might have to tell someone they suck at something, then you know how I feel right now. It's awkward and uncomfortable, and I want to kick Vi for not giving me some kind of warning, but she's also doing me a huge favor so I guess I'll have to hope he's as good as she says. "Why don't you play while we get set up, and we'll see if the music is a match for tonight?"

I still give Vi the stink-eye, but she just winks and laughs. Bitch.

We get to work, me, Tate and Vi, while Jasmine and Nicole go into the bedroom to change. Tate has had all the alcohol brought up and is helping Vi set up the bar while I work to make the room festive, fun and sexy for the party.

But my hands still, my breath hitches, when Chad begins to sing. It's a haunting melody, and his voice is hypnotic. I turn to watch him as he strums his guitar, his beautiful falsetto voice filling the room. Vi and Tate have stopped too and are just as lost in his performance as I am. When he finishes, I clap the loudest, truly blown away by his talent. "That was amazing. You are incredible. I don't know if it's the right vibe for tonight, but I will find a way to get you in, maybe toward the end when things are quieting down. Do you perform at other events?"

His shy grin fills with joy. "I've been trying to. It takes some connections that I don't have, but Vi has been spreading the word about me, which has helped bring in a few gigs."

"You'd be a hit at a few bachelorette parties we're planning this summer. Give me your number, and let's see what we can do."

His eyes light up. "Thank you so much. Vi said you were amazing, and she was right."

"Vi is biased," I say, but I'm pleased at the compliment. I check my watch, and my heart ramps up again. "The guys will be here soon. We've got to get everything finished up."

Tate sets up speakers and puts on our standard playlist of popular music that keeps the energy high. Jasmine and Nicole both have their own music they dance to, but they'll stay in the bedroom until it's time for their dances.

When the first person knocks on the door, I'm just finishing up the food platters provided by the hotel.

Everything looks perfect, and I smile, swipe my lips with Russian Red lipstick and open the door to our guests.

My heart stops, and I don't even acknowledge the groom and his other friends, because standing before me is Sebastian Donovan.

EIGHT

Cigars and Strippers

My mouth falls open, but I quickly shut it, channeling all my professionalism as I pull my eyes from Sebastian to the groom, who is talking to me.

"So nice to meet you in person," Dan says, hand extended to shake.

I smile, grip his hand firmly and open the door for him and his friends. "Come in. Everything's ready for your big night."

His friends tumble into the room, filling it with testosterone. We've already dimmed the lights, turned up the music, and a few guys head straight to the bar, whether for drinks or to admire Vi, I'm not sure, but I can see her turning on the charm as she mixes and serves and flirts just enough to keep them coming back.

I expect to see Chad a bit jealous, but he's having just as much fun talking, laughing and serving drinks. My estimation of him increases as I turn my attention back to Dan.

"I hope you find everything as anticipated." I lead him to a special area where I've set up a smoking lounge with the finest Cuban cigars money (and a few well-placed connections) can buy. "As you requested. I think you'll find these to your liking."

He picks a cigar up and lifts it to his nose, inhaling deeply. "A 1989 Punch Punch. These are extremely hard to come by and one of the most coveted Cuban cigars around. I don't know how you managed this."

I laugh. "This is nothing. You should see what some clients have requested. It was my pleasure."

He's a handsome man with dark eyes, blond hair and a kind smile. He hasn't even glanced at Vi, which doesn't surprise me. Contrary to Hollywood tropes, most grooms don't ogle other women during their bachelor party. Most of them spend the whole night talking about their bride, and I can tell he won't be any different.

"Janet, my fiancée, wanted to use you too, but since I found you first, I won."

"I hope she's having a good time," I say, meaning it. Some day I hope to grow our business enough that we can take on two parties in one night, just for this reason. But we're not quite there yet.

He checks his phone, smiles and texts something, and I know he's probably going to be texting her all night while his friends and her friends celebrate.

Dan settles in with a cigar, using a cigar cutter to nip off the end and then lighting it. The room begins to smell spicy with a hint of vanilla, and I don't mind it. Cigar smoke has a richer quality than cigarettes, which I can't stand, and I enjoy the sweet, smoky atmosphere it creates.

I'm doing my best to avoid looking in Sebastian's direction, a sick feeling forming in the pit of my stomach as I realize I'll have to spend the whole evening pretending we are nothing to each other.

The other men have settled into chairs we've arranged around the room, scattered with small tables for their food and drink. Tate turns down the music so I can introduce my staff and myself and give them a brief reminder of what the evening will include—and what it will not.

When I give my standard disclaimer about no sex, no touching, no propositioning the dancers, a surly looking man with a goatee and small dark eyes actually "boos" me.

"We didn't come here to look. We came here for some action. That's what these parties are supposed to be about."

"What's your name, sir?" I ask. Tate is walking over to my side to create an impression of "don't fuck with us," I'm sure. I don't mind. He is the bouncer if things get too wild, which has only happened once.

"Henry," he says. And by his slurred words and clouded eyes, I can tell he's already been drinking. Great. Don't you just love a drunken man in a room full of still-sober people? Yeah, me neither.

"Henry," I keep a smile on my face and my voice conversational and light, "we made it clear to Dan when he chose us that we don't provide that particular service. If you're looking for companionship, there are other places on the Strip that will accommodate."

He frowns, his face sullen, but he doesn't argue, and I'm glad he's not making more of a scene. I give a look to my brother, and he nods. We'll both be keeping an eye on the guy.

Tate turns the music back up and puts on a set for our dancers.

Jasmine comes out first, her body covered in ribbons of fabric that I know will come off one by one as the song progresses.

We've created a pseudo stage for them, complete with a removable pole. We hired these two dancers in particular because of their remarkable skill on the pole. It never ceases to wow our clients.

Jasmine moves around the room, seducing each man with her eyes, with her swaying hips, as she pulls the ribbons off her dress, revealing bits of skin with each discarded cloth.

Most of the men in the room can't turn their eyes from her. Except Chad, who keeps glancing at Vi; Tate, who keeps his eyes sweeping the room; the groom, who's still texting his wife-to-be…

And Sebastian, who hasn't stopped staring at me since he arrived.

I can't avoid his gaze any longer, and so I turn my eyes to him, admiring his chiseled features, the way his body fills his jeans to perfection, the way he looks at me as if he wants to eat me.

My body burns with the same need I always have at the thought or sight of him, but I'm also angry. Angry he's here—and you and I both know it's not an accident—and angry that he won't accept no for an answer. And, if I'm being honest, angry that I don't want him to accept my no. Totally lame, am I right? I suck.

As Jasmine finishes up her dance, Nicole comes in, and the music changes to something more upbeat. She's dressed in an exotic belly-dancing costume, and she begins her strip tease.

By the end, both dancers are in a bra and panties with high heels. The men are nearly salivating. Vi keeps plying them with drink, and I make sure to walk the hors d'oeuvre tray around so they get something in their stomach.

When I lean over to serve the belligerent Henry, he breathes his liquored breath into my face and speaks in a hushed voice. "If they're not available, what about you? You could be a stripper with that body and a model with that face. I'd do you, and I'd pay nicely for it." He holds up a wad of cash and puts it in my hands. I take it, put it into our tip jar, and smile. "Thank you, but the answer is still no."

His face turns mean, but I leave him to serve the others, who also offer tips, without the propositions, and our jar fills with money that will go to Vi and the dancers. Tate and I never take tips collected at the parties. If the groom or bride want to tip us directly afterwards, that's fine.

When the music shifts again, the room turns foggy with white smoke from a smoke machine, and lights come on in different colors under the smoke, giving it a haunted dream-like look. Nicole dances around with ribbons as Jasmine begins a pole dance that is nothing short of athletic in its beauty. At one point she is actually walking on the ceiling, using only her arms to support her on the pole.

I can hear one of the men gasp, and I know they're as impressed as everyone is. The show is sexy, classy and amazing.

When it ends, they both reveal their breasts to clapping and catcalling, and they offer lap dances to those who want to pay more. I remind the men of the rules and look for Tate, knowing he'll keep an eye on things as I step away to call room service for dessert to be sent up.

I'm alone in the bedroom when the door opens. I expect it to be Tate or Vi. I want it to be Sebastian.

It's Henry. And now he's really drunk.

He leers at me as he stalks toward me. He's got a good one hundred pounds on me and is much taller. I know some karate, so I'm not too scared—hey, a girl's gotta be able to defend herself in a city like this—but my heart still jumps into my throat. "Henry, please return to the other guests. This room is private."

"Which makes it perfect for what I want. You took my money, bitch. Now I'm going to take what I paid for."

He's about to grab me as I raise my knee to catch him in the balls when the door opens again, and Sebastian is there, looking like he's ready to kill someone.

He grabs Henry and pulls him away from me. "What the fuck are you doing in here with her?"

Henry unwisely gloats. "None of your fucking business."

"It is now," he says and punches the man in the jaw. My first thought is, holy shit. My second is immediate concern for Sebastian's hands. He's a surgeon. Punching someone isn't a great idea when your whole career relies on your hands.

But he doesn't seem to care about his hands or his career. He's about to punch him again, but Tate joins us with a face full of apology. "Let's get this guy out of here," he says to Sebastian, who visibly calms down and nods.

They both escort Henry to the door, and Sebastian makes a call, securing a cab for the man through the concierge of the hotel.

When Tate closes and locks the door behind Henry, I finally breathe normally. The music has stopped, I realize, and all the party guests are staring at us.

"I apologize for the brief interruption. Who would like another dance from our amazing dancers? This time to live music?"

The men nod eagerly, and I give a nod to Chad to do his thing. He looks about ready to piss himself, but he grabs his guitar and sits to the side of the stage as he begins strumming his guitar.

I know Jasmine and Nicole will find ways to improvise this. They're that good. And they don't disappoint. They create a very sexy, very sultry dance that's almost story like in its presentation as Chad sings.

The men are mesmerized, and I use the distraction to make sure Dan is okay.

He apologizes before I have a chance to say anything. "I shouldn't have invited him, but he's my cousin, and my parents twisted my arm. I'm so sorry."

I smile. "It's okay. We're used to it. No biggie." This is a lie, but it makes him feel better.

"I'll pay for any inconvenience he posed."

"Just enjoy the rest of your night," I say.

It seems that he does. The party goes late into the early morning before the men tire and start leaving one by one.

I'm dead on my feet as the last one departs. I look around but don't see Sebastian, and I shove away the disappointment that I didn't get to talk to him when he left. Vi and Chad leave after that, and Tate packs up what he brought and gives the dancers a ride home. "I've got to stay and clean up, but I'll be home in a little bit. You don't need to come back. I've got this covered," I tell him.

"Are you sure?" He doesn't look convinced.

"Yup. Get the girls home." I hand him the tip jar. "Split this up with them and save some for Vi. This should make them happy."

He kisses my cheek. "Will do, sis. Be safe and don't stay out too late."

I give him my best wide-eyed innocence look. "Who me? Never."

I can still hear his laughter down the hall as he leaves.

Once alone, the weight of exhaustion hits me, but I still have work to do. I'm cleaning up cups and wiping up spills when the hotel door opens.

I turn, startled. Tate and I should be the only ones with the key.

But apparently not.

Sebastian has one too, it seems.

NINE

The Remaking of Kacie Michaels

"What are you doing here?" I ask him, my body too still, frozen in place as I gape at him. I hate him for showing up here. I want to slap him for refusing to sign the papers. And I'm pissed off because, despite all that, I want to kiss him.

He takes long strides toward me, his body thrumming with pent-up energy, his eyes devouring me. "I came to help you clean up."

His answer disarms me. "What?"

"I came to help you clean up," he repeats. "From the party."

I must look like someone who doesn't understand words at all anymore, because he frowns and looks around at the mess, gesturing with his hands. "Clean. Up." He says slowly.

I can't help but laugh despite myself. "I get it. Sorry, that just…surprised me. It wasn't what I was expecting."

"What were you expecting?" he asks. He grabs a trash bag and starts tossing plates and napkins in.

I shrug, not willing to turn down help when I'm dead on my feet, and start taking down the decorations. "I don't know. I guess, something more carnal."

He pauses in his cleaning and smiles in that devilish way he has. "That comes later. After your job is done and you can relax and fully enjoy those carnal delights."

I ignore the tingling sensation trailing down my spine as I continue cleaning the hotel room. "What were you doing at this party?" I ask, but I already suspect the answer.

"Who do you think referred you?" He takes the full trash bag from my hands and ties it off, then places it next to the door. "You wouldn't return my calls, so I had to find a way to see you."

I steel myself, resolve flooding me even as my passion for him simmers. "So you thought meddling with my business was the way to my heart? This isn't a hobby for me," I say too loudly. "This is my career. My livelihood. You had no right."

"I would never do anything to damage your business," he says. "It was a legitimate reference, and Dan had a great time. He and his friends will definitely be spreading the word about Hitched and you. And I kept my distance during the party so you could work."

I take a breath and realize he's right. He didn't hurt my business or damage me in any way. Was it manipulative? Yes. But not worth getting this upset about. He gave me a client. That hardly makes him a bad guy.

And now he's emptying beer bottles into the hotel sink and wiping down suspicious looking fluids from the table.

"Thank you for the referral," I say, once my temper's checked. "And thank you for your help tonight."

"You're welcome."

I keep looking for something more to clean, but the hotel room is nearly spotless by the time we're both done. There's nothing left to do but face him.

Before I can object, he pulls me into his arms and claims my mouth with his. He tastes of wine and cigars, and my body responds to him even as my mind tries to put the halt on the sexy times.

My mind finally wins, and I push him away. I'm out of breath, and my brain is cloudy with desire, but I force reason into the moment. "I can't do this again," I say.

He caresses my face with his hand, running a long finger down my cheek and jawline. "I don't think either of us has a choice."

He dips his head, his lips pressing into my neck, a flick of his tongue setting my skin aflame, and I groan even as I curse him for everything he's making me feel.

But I don't resist. Because I want him too much. These last few weeks have been miserable. I haven't been able to get him out of my mind. Maybe this will be it, one more dance before we end it for real.

And by dance, I of course mean hot, wild sex.

His hands are exploring my body, and I let go of him to pull off my blouse and unzip my skirt. They fall to the floor, and I'm standing in front of him in nothing but black lace and silk and high heels.

I reach to take his shirt off, but he drops to his knees instead and begins trailing kisses down my belly, his hands on my hips and ass, fingers pressing into my flesh.

When his tongue runs over my panties, teasing my pussy, my head falls back, and my hands dig into his hair, gripping him as he releases my hip and uses a finger to slide the silk fabric away. This time the firm pressure of his mouth comes in direct contact with my clit, and I moan.

My fantasies didn't do him justice. My own fingers could never compete with the feel of his tongue between my legs, eating my pussy.

He slides a finger inside me, then two. Long, strong fingers that know exactly where to touch to make me weak.

I'm near the edge of an orgasm, my muscles clenching, body ready to unravel, but he stops, pulling his fingers out of me, the air cool against the flesh wet from his tongue. I nearly scream.

"I've been imagining this since the night at the restaurant," he says, his voice husky and eyes filled with desire.

I don't want to admit the same, so I remain silent, still poised on the edge of climax, body reluctantly unwinding.

He stands, rubbing himself against me as he does, his cock pressing against his jeans so hard I worry it will break open the zipper. "I need you," he says, then he puts an arm around my shoulder and another under my knees and picks me up, carrying me into the bedroom.

I feel light, sexy, safe, and so fucking horny I will surely die if he does not finish what he started.

He lays me gently on the bed and peels off my panties, then moves his hands up my body, freeing my breasts from my bra. Standing back, he admires me for a moment, and I spread my legs, giving him full view of everything I'm offering.

"This is going to be difficult if you don't take off some clothes," I say. "We're not having movie sex. Real life fucking requires some skin-to-skin contact."

He smiles, and it lights up his face, softening the strong jaw, and that smile undoes me.

"Patience, darling. I'm memorizing you first."

But I'm not a patient girl, so I move between his legs and unbutton those jeans that don't look like they can take much more cock. Once he's free, I take him into my mouth, and it's his turn to moan and grab my hair. I suck deeply, stroking his base, running my fingernails gently over his balls as I move my mouth around his huge cock. It fills my mouth, and I can't take him all the way in, but I try. I can tell it drives him crazy.

And then I stop, just as I can feel pressure building for him.

He looks down at me, a glint in his eyes, and I smile sweetly. "Sucks, doesn't it? Horny yet?"

Without a word, he pulls off the rest of his clothes, and I realize I'd forgotten just how fucking gorgeous this man is. I'm not a shallow person. There's more to a guy then just his looks or cock size. But come on, we can be honest with each other. The fact that he's sculpted like Adonis isn't exactly a drawback, you know?

He pushes me to the bed, but I want control this time. I flip him over and straddle him, my tits brushing against his mouth as I rub my pussy against his cock without letting him fill me. The teasing is hard on us both. I want him just as badly as he wants me, but I also want him to suffer, just a little.

I smile, biting my lip, as I take him in just enough to make him groan and clutch my hips with his hands. Holding myself above him with my legs, I move up and down, fucking just the tip of his cock as we hold eye contact.

"You're evil, you know that?" he says through clenched teeth. I can tell he's using all his self-control not to shove his hips into mine and impale himself in me fully. I admire his restraint.

Mine is fading. I want to feel him. All of him.

"Serves you right," I tell him. And then I sink onto him, taking every inch of his hard cock into me. One smooth motion that makes us both cry out.

He's so goddamn big he stretches me, and it feels incredible. I enjoy being in control like this, riding him, moving my hips and my body as he matches me with his rhythm, his hands still on my waist. We slam into each other, our eyes locked together, our bodies moving as one.

I thought we'd just start in this position and then change, but there's a chemistry here that neither of us wants to break. It's not just the physical pleasure of feeling him inside me. The way our bodies are connected, the way we are getting lost in each other…I don't want it to end.

I slow my movements, riding him with less urgency to make this moment last longer. My mind is filled with only him, us, this moment, and I am his completely.

When we come, it is as one, and I am remade in that moment, remade into someone new. Remade into someone who can't imagine not seeing Sebastian Donovan again.

TEN

Compromises

Laying here with him like this, with actual memories together during periods of sobriety, I am beginning to imagine a future with this man. Something more than just sex. And I can't believe I'm about to admit this, but I think I'm going to take his offer. I'll put aside the annulment and date him for the summer. After that, well, we can cross that bridge then, if a summer hasn't blown it into bits and pieces.

"I have one condition," he says.

I have no idea what he's talking about. I lift my head off his chest and stare into his cobalt blue eyes. "What?"

"To signing the annulment papers. I have a condition."

My heart skips a beat. It's like he can read my mind; only if he could, he wouldn't be offering to sign the papers now. I feel…sad. It's silly, I know. This is really what I want. Even if we are truly meant to be, which I'm totally not convinced of yet, that doesn't mean I want to start our life off with a drunken elopement I can't remember. Still. There's sadness. Shut up about it, okay?

"What's your condition?" I sit up in bed, naked and unashamed. I never got the point of being shy after someone's already seen you naked.

"I still want the summer," he says. "With you. A one hundred percent commitment. At the end of the summer, we'll call it quits if you still want to."

I pause. It's basically the same deal, so why are we even talking about this?

He sees the question in my eyes and smiles. "I'm not an asshole, Kacie. You can get the annulment with or without my signature, but I don't want you thinking I'm trying to coerce you into anything. You can still say no, even now. I just hope you won't."

"I'm afraid I can't be what you want and need," I tell him honestly. "You're ready for the marriage and kids, which makes sense. You've got your career and your life pretty well defined. Me? I'm not even close. I'm still a mess trying to piece together the life I want. I'm not ready to give it all up, even for someone as amazing as you."

He smiles. "I'm amazing, huh?"

I throw a pillow at him. "Is that all you took out of what I just said?"

He sits up and faces me. "No. I hear you. But I'm not sure I understand. I'm not asking for kids. Yet. I'm not asking you to give up anything. I'm just asking for you."

My heart beats wildly, and I want to throw myself at him, but I know who I am and what I'm capable of. And I know what this decision would cost me. "My mom thought she could have it all. So did my sister. But as soon as they got married, they got pregnant, and who do you think had to make the sacrifices to take care of the kids or cook dinner or clean house or stay home with sick kids? Don't get me wrong, I love my mom and my sister, but I don't want to be them."

He shakes his head. "I'm not asking that of you."

"I know you don't think you are, but this," I flap my arms around between us, "whatever this is, it's not casual, is it? We got married our first night together. I don't remember how or why, but I've been drunk before and never ended up married. And I can't stop thinking about you. I can't stop imagining you in my life. It scares the hell out me. You're a doctor. I plan bachelor parties. Whose career do you think will trump whose when we have kids and one of us has to stay home? Mine, obviously, because saving the lives of children is way more important than planning parties, and I can't be with someone whose life will always trump mine."

"My career will never trump yours. And we can have this without the kids. They invented this thing called birth control; as a doctor, I assure you it's pretty effective. Just give it a shot, Kacie. Give us a shot. It doesn't have to lead anywhere you don't want it to."

I can't believe I'm about to say this, but…"Yes. Okay. Yes. I'll give you a summer."

I say yes, because how can I say no? I'd just obsess about him anyways, so I might as well spend time with him. Maybe we'll get sick of each other after a few weeks, and I can go back to the carefree business owner I was the night I met him.

But that fear is still in me. That fear that I will lose myself in this man and stop being everything that makes me Kacie Michaels. The fear that I will indeed become my mother, and once that happens, it'll already too late.

I can give him the summer, as promised.

But I'm not sure I can give him a lifetime.

ELEVEN

Dinner Dates

This doesn't have to change me. It's just a casual dating relationship, that's all. If I keep telling myself this often enough, maybe I'll believe it. Maybe it'll even become true.

It's only been twenty-four hours since I've seen the sexy doctor, and I'm already acting like a teen with the worst crush of her life.

Vi snaps her fingers in my face. "Earth to Kacie. You going to join us at all tonight, or should we get you and your thoughts a private room?"

"Funny," I say, but I smile because she's right. I'm being an asshole. "What were we talking about?"

Vi sighs as only she can sigh. "Chad. Things are heating up between us. He's over at my place all the time. We're talking about moving in together."

My eyes widen, but our waiter comes to refill our drinks, so I keep my thoughts silent until he leaves. Tate has a date tonight with his new girlfriend, so Vi and I decided to make it a girls' night. Something we haven't done in a while. Contrary to what you might think, given our respective jobs, we're pretty tame for the most part.

Tonight we're at a little Italian place we like to go to when we feel like living dangerously with carbs.

I look down at my plate, piled high with what has to be the best cheese ravioli and garlic bread in the universe. It's definitely a dangerous night. Especially since I also have my eye on the seven layer chocolate cake this place is famous for.

Once we're alone again, I give Vi my best shocked face. "You just met the guy. Isn't it a bit soon to move in together?"

She smirks at me. "Says the woman who married her date the first night."

"And look what a mess I'm in because of it."

She shoves a fork full of spaghetti into her mouth and chews for a few moments before speaking. "I'm not saying I'm doing it. But you have to admit, he's a pretty great guy."

I nod. "I'll give you that. And man, does he have a voice on him. He really should record an album."

"I've been telling him the same thing. He's nervous. He hasn't gotten much support from family, and he's worried he'll end up a failure if he pursues his music seriously."

I take another bite of my dinner and wash it down with a delicious red wine. I would have thought Vi would end up with someone strong, confident. Someone who could match her strength and wits. I know she likes to be the Dom at work, but I'm still surprised she seems to prefer that role in her romantic ties as well. It doesn't seem to fit her, but it's not for me to judge what should make her happy. Chad is a great guy. I got no red flags from him. "I hope he gets over that. I know it's hard to run in a different direction than your family wants you to. But it's our lives. We only live once, and we have to make the most of it."

"Unless reincarnation is true," she says, always the combative. "Then we get lots of chances."

"They don't count, since most of us can't really remember them," I counter.

When dessert is brought out, I'm so stuffed I can hardly breathe, but I am also committed to this cake and will finish it regardless of the gastrointestinal price I'll have to pay later.

"Where's Doctor Dreamy tonight?" she asks.

"Working."

As if on cue, my phone buzzes, and I look down at the text and blush.

I'm leaving work, and all I can think about is how tight your pussy felt around my cock last night. I need you. Soon.

I text back quickly, knowing I'm being rude to Vi, but I can't resist replying to him.

How soon are we talking?

Vi looks questioningly at my phone, and I grin. "He's done for the night," I explain.

Vi wags her eyebrows. "And I'm gathering by your pink cheeks that those aren't just regular texts?"

I squeeze my lips shut and look down as another text comes in.

Where are you right now?

"I don't know what you mean," I say, totally unconvincingly.

Out to dinner with Vi. And my panties are wet for you right now. I want to suck your cock again.

Vi reaches over and grabs the phone from me before I can stop her. Her eyes widen as she reads our sexting. "Oh, your husband-boyfriend is naughty."

"He's not my—" but I stop, because, well, I guess he is. This is all so confusing.

Vi types something into my phone and hits send, then tosses the phone back to me. "You're welcome."

I read what she wrote. It's the address to our restaurant and an invitation to come pick me up. "What are you doing? We're supposed to hang out at my place after this."

She shakes her head. "I'm not going to stand between you and true lust. Go freshen up. He'll likely be here soon."

I hurry from the table and find the restroom. As I'm reapplying some lipstick, the door opens, and Sebastian Donovan strides in like he owns the place. I expected him in scrubs, but it makes sense that he wouldn't wear them around town. Instead, he's got on jeans and a blue cotton shirt that brings out his eyes. His dark hair is disheveled, and his eyes look tired, but his smile devastates me.

"I think you need some training on which bathroom the boys are supposed to use," I tell him.

"Separate bathrooms are trite," he says, and then pulls me to him and kisses me deeply.

He tastes like mint, and I melt into him as he holds me close.

"Do you have a thing for bathrooms?" I ask, when our kisses pause.

"No, just a thing for you."

When a woman walks in and sees us, I blush, and he smiles. She just stares.

Sebastian, without saying a word, guides me out of the bathroom and through the restaurant to my table. Vi is standing, her purse in hand, and the bill has already been paid for our dinner.

She smiles brightly at me. "You two have fun. Don't do anything I wouldn't do."

Sebastian frowns, but I laugh, because there's not much Vi won't do. Except dishes. She really hates doing dishes.

I kiss her cheek, thank her for the night and we promise to get together again soon. "Tell Chad I said hi," I say as we walk out of the restaurant and go our separate ways. I'd driven here with her, and I'm apparently leaving with Sebastian.

"Where would you like me to fuck you tonight?" he asks.

His words send a shiver through my body, and I think for a moment before responding. "Your house."

TWELVE

Blowjobs

He pauses. "My house?"

I nod. "You asked me for the summer. I'm giving you the summer. But that means tit for tat. You've seen my house; I want to see yours."

"Fair enough," he says.

He holds my hand as we continue walking to his car. His hand practically swallows mine. It's big and warm, and when I think about how it feels to have those fingers roaming my body, something clenches inside me, and I hope that he doesn't live too far away.

The night is surprisingly cool, and I press in closer to him, enjoying his warmth and the chill in the air.

Normally I skip car rides. They are usually pretty boring, wouldn't you agree? But this drive is anything but boring.

It starts with his right hand on my knee. My skin burns at his touch, greedy for more.

As he drives, his hand moves up my thigh, under my skirt and between my legs. I suck in my breath as his fingers brush over my panties, teasing my pussy with gentle movement.

"Wait," I say, "I want to fuck in your bed."

"And we will, but I need your pussy now, Kacie." Grinning, he massages my clit through the fabric.

"Sebastian…" My words cut off as I get lost in the ecstasy of his fingers.

"Yes?"

"More."

His fingers slip under satin and penetrate me.

I bite down on my lip, stopping myself from crying out.

"Don't hold back, darling. Never hold back with me," he says.

And I let myself cry out. "Fuck. Sebastian." His fingers feel so good, but there's one more thing I want to know. "Did I—"

"Darling, we can talk later, but right now, I need something from you."

"Yes?"

"I need you lips around my cock, Kacie."

I want to finish my question, but my hand trails up his muscled leg to his already hard cock, and I remember how good he tastes.

"Kacie, I need you."

Fuck. That settles it.

As he fingers my pussy, rubbing against my clit only enough to tease without release, I unzip his jeans and free his cock. As we're stopped at a red light, I lean over his lap and take him into my mouth. He moans, one hand between my legs still as the other grips my head.

"Fuck, Kacie. You know how crazy you make me?"

I don't answer, because my mouth is full of cock, but I suck harder, stroking and licking as I look up at him.

When the light turns green, cars behind us honk, and he pulls off the road as I continue to suck and lick. I can feel his body tense, and his finger inside me moves harder, pushing me deeper into a spiral of pleasure even as I bring him to the brink.

"I need you to take me as deep as you can," he says.

I take him almost completely, his cock filling my throat. Then I pull back a little. And with another lick I send him over the edge. His come is hot in my mouth, and I swallow it all, licking the rest off his shaft and tip as his fingertips dig into my scalp.

When I sit up, he shudders, his smile slow and sexy, and continues playing with my pussy, rubbing my clit until I too climax, my muscles tensing, body going tight as a wave of pleasure floods me.

We're silent for several moments, holding each other, lost in our own thoughts. "Wow," is all I can say.

"My sentiments exactly," he says.

We tug our clothes back in place, and he starts the car and pulls back into traffic.

There's been something on my mind since the nigh we met, and so I ask the question I really want to know, have been curious about since I woke up in his arms and realized we were married.

"The night we got married…did we? Did I? Did you? Um…did we say the 'L' word at any point?" Oh God, I sound like a moron.

"Which 'L' word would that be?" I can hear the teasing in his voice, and I know I deserve it.

"You know what word I'm talking about. Did we profess our love to each other?"

"Yes." His answer is simple. Short. Incomplete. Because now I have too many other questions.

"Did you mean it?" I hold my breath waiting for his answer.

"I don't say anything I don't mean."

That's a yes. That means he loves me, or he did that night. My heart flip-flops.

"Why did we get married? It seems so unlikely, for either us."

"I can only speak for myself. I married you because I knew that night, and I know this even now, that you are someone I don't want to live without. My mother always said when it comes to choosing your mate, don't pick someone you can live with. Choose someone you can't live without. That's what I did when I married you."

THIRTEEN

Home Sweet Home

He lives about twenty-five minutes from the Strip, in a larger house than I would have imagined for a single man living alone. At least, I assume he lives alone. I have to remind myself that despite having married the man, and despite all the amazing sex, I know frighteningly little about him. I guess that's what he thinks this summer will be about—getting to know each other. For me, it's about getting over him. I'm convinced that if I spend enough time with him, his flaws will show, and the bloom will fade. When that happens, I'll be able to put him out of my mind, and heart, once and for all.

But of course, the more he talks, the more I learn about him, the more my heart resists imagining a life without him.

Large palm trees stand sentinel in his lush, green front yard. Lit globes line the walkway to his front door, with bushes trimming the path. The impossibly green grass is dotted with terra cotta colored boulders and stones, and boasts at least three different breeds of trees in addition to the palms. The house itself is Spanish in style, with touches of Moroccan architecture. The dark red tile roof and thick stucco walls gives the house an inviting feeling that evokes images of family and friends.

He pulls into the four-car garage, and I follow him into a spacious kitchen fit for a chef with cast iron pots and pans hanging over an island in the middle. "Do you cook?" I ask.

"I guess you'll find out when I make you breakfast in the morning." He winks at me, and my stomach flutters.

I wish I'd brought a change of clothes, but it won't be the first time I do the walk of shame in the morning, and it probably won't be the last. Though I hear women are reclaiming this term to counteract the prevalence of our slut-shaming culture. Now it's the "strut of pride." I like that better, though I still hate being stuck in last night's clothes. Time to start carrying an overnight bag with me.

"Welcome to my home," he says, clutching my hand close to him as we step into his living room. It's huge, with a wide screen television taking up most of one wall and comfortable leather couches and chairs arranged strategically for conversation or entertainment. The walls are high, the ceilings tall and there's a fireplace in the center of it all, one that takes real wood and looks well used. An eclectic mix of art pieces hang from white walls, giving splashes of color to the space. In a corner sits a black grand piano. "Do you play?" I ask.

"Not anymore," he says. Before I can ask why, he continues. "Would you like a tour?"

"I'd love one."

He takes me through the rest of the house, where I learn that his office desk is the only messy part of his life, that he likes swimming in his Olympic-sized pool that has a crazy amount of landscaping around it to give it a feel of being in the tropics, that he has enough guest rooms to house several families, and that he enjoys reading outside on his shaded patio. I know this because he left a few books on the table by the most comfortable looking chair. I sneak a glance at the titles and roll my eyes. Medical books, of course. I'd have romance novels.

We end the tour in his bedroom, which is dominated by a king bed facing another fireplace and has a nook for reading or watching television on another larger than life screen. His bathroom is to die for, with a sunken, jetted tub, a shower with multiple heads, and a walk-in closet that I might have to steal, at least for a few months.

I whistle. "We're definitely spending more time at your house than mine this summer."

He laughs. "I normally find it too much space for just one person." He wraps his arms around me and pulls me against his body. "But with you here, I can imagine some possibilities."

"Why did you buy something so big just for you?" This house must have cost close to a million.

His face darkens, and he looks away. "I bought it with someone. We planned on starting a family here, but things didn't work out."

My heart lurches. I'd like to say it's because I feel his pain, and it saddens me, but if I'm being honest, it's also some jealousy. Even though I don't want that kind of life, and I hate this about myself right now. I'm jealous that he started building it with someone else. I'm a bitch, I know.

"Were you married?" He'd said he'd never been married.

"No. Engaged."

"What happened?"

His eyes fix on me again, and he smiles. "Let's not talk about the past. It ended a few years ago, and I'm over it. I'd rather focus on the present. With you."

I understand and let the conversation rest as we go back downstairs. I notice something in the living room I didn't see before. A wall with framed art, but not done by professionals. "Who drew these?" I ask. There are pictures of rainbows and ponies and many drawings of what looks like a doctor holding the hand of a child.

"My patients. They often draw pictures for me, and I always frame them and hang them here, then take photos of their art displays to show them later. They love seeing their artwork featured like this. It raises their spirits."

"They're beautiful. They must really love you."

He smiles wistfully. "They're incredible kids. To go through what they do with such a positive outlook... they're the bravest people I know."

I walk toward him, my heart swelling at his kindness and dedication to the kids he helps, and I wrap my arms around him. "You're pretty amazing, you know that?"

He responds by kissing me, then smiling. "What do you want to do now? There's that bath you were eyeing upstairs, or would you rather skinny dip in the pool first?"

I weigh the two options, but the lure of swimming naked is too much. He's found my weakness and exploited it, the bastard.

I unbutton my blouse and shrug it off my shoulders, then pull down my skirt, kicking it to the side.

He breathes in sharply as I slip off my bra, his eyes glued to my body.

Once I'm completely naked, I grin at him. "Which way to the pool?"

FOURTEEN

Pool Party for Three

I tease him as I slowly walk outside, swaying my hips and tossing back flirty smiles.

He catches up to me and drops his hands to my waist. His skin is hot, and I can't wait to get him naked and into the water with me.

The air outside caresses me as we step into his tropical backyard. I love swimming naked, but so rarely have the chance to do it in a big city like Las Vegas. Without wasting another moment, I kick off my heels—the only remaining clothing I have on—and dive with perfect form into the deep end of the pool.

My head pushes through the surface, and I smile at him. "Come on in; the water's great."

He laughs. "You're delightful and unexpected, Ms. Michaels."

"Come join me in all this unexpected delight," I say.

With the ease of a man comfortable with his own body, he sheds his clothing, and I watch with desire. In the moonlight and the flickers of colorful lights that have lit up the pool area, his body is aglow in splendor, setting off the tight bulges of his muscles. His cock is long and hard and at full attention, and I'm ready for it to be inside of me.

He dives in and swims to me, pulling me against him while keeping us both afloat. I wrap my legs around him, our bodies molding together underwater.

"You look magical in moonlight," he tells me, then kisses me before I can reply. The kiss is light, soft, teasing. Then it deepens, claiming my lips, my tongue, making my body shiver from the pressure building inside of me.

"Wait a moment," he says, turning away. "I need to get a condom."

Shaking, I grab his shoulder, unsure that I should say what I'm about to say. "I know we've been using condoms since that first night, but I'm on birth control, and I don't have any STDS, and I'm sure you—"

"I don't." He stares at me, serious.

"Then I want to feel you inside of me."

He pauses, then nods. "I've been imagining this." His words surprise me, but why should they? Haven't I been imagining the same thing?

Perhaps I'm scared by the idea that I care about him just as much as he cares about me. That at the end of summer, I might not be ready to let go.

As I straddle him, he moves us closer to the shallow end until his feet touch the bottom. I settle onto him, his cock teasing my pussy as we come closer and closer together.

When he places his hands on my hips and pushes me onto his throbbing cock, I am lost in him.

"God, Kacie, you feel so fucking good."

"Fuck me harder," I moan in response, riding him as he thrusts into me. His cock feels hot and hard and amazing, and I want to feel every inch of it. I've always been careful; this is my first time without a condom. I've never felt closer to anyone before, never *been* closer to anyone, and it feels better than anything I've ever imagined.

"You like how my cock feels?" he asks, slowing down.

I nod, biting my lip.

"Then say it. I need you to say it."

"I love how your cock feels."

He smiles. "Good. Now ride it hard. Ride it hard until I come inside you."

We move our bodies together, in small, desperate friction as we each strive for deeper, harder, more…He cups my ass with his hands as I use my legs to ride him, holding onto his shoulders as they flex under my hands.

He fills me, stretches me, makes me feel alive and present and free, and I never want it to end, but at the same time I want the release, crave the explosion of pleasure deep in belly. I feel it building. I know I can get there with his cock inside me, with my tender nipples rubbing against his chest with each thrust.

Our eyes are locked, his cobalt eyes peering into my soul. I am shattered into a million pieces, like stars in the sky, as the orgasm that had been building explodes inside me along with his cock.

He holds me close as my body collapses against him.

His voice is husky when he speaks. "That was—"

"—Amazing," I finish, my voice also deeper, raw with sensuality.

I feel the loss of him as he pulls out. Colorful lights flicker at the bottom of the pool, and I dive back underwater to clear my head, swimming a lap just for the pleasure.

When I swim back to him, I smile with a challenge. "Race you."

He raises an eyebrow in surprise. "I do use this pool regularly. Are you sure you want to lose this early in our relationship?"

I laugh. "You're the one who should ask himself that question before accepting the challenge."

What I don't tell him is that I was on the swim team in college. I'll let him figure that out on his own.

We push off, and despite myself, I'm impressed at his speed. I focus, pumping my arms and legs harder, moving faster, determined to win no matter what.

He somehow gets ahead of me, but only by a fraction, and I've caught up by the time we reach the end of the pool to turn around. My turn pushes me ahead by the tips of my fingers, but I push my body to keep the edge and extend it.

I will win.

And I do. By less than a second, I reach the starting point before him.

We are both winded and breathing hard, so it takes a moment before I see that he's not looking at me but at something behind me.

And he doesn't look happy.

I turn around and look up at one of the most beautiful women I've ever seen, standing near the pool looking down at us with wide eyes and a frown.

"Sebastian," she says. "Is this any way to greet your fiancée?"

FIFTEEN

Concerns of the Heart

"Who the fuck are you?" The words are out of my mouth before I can consider how appropriate they might be, but whatever, I'm naked. Sebastian is naked. This woman isn't averting her eyes or even pretending to feign embarrassment. She's just staring, her frown now turned to disdain, and I hate her immediately.

Sebastian grabs a towel from the side of the pool and tosses it to me. It's now wet, but I cover myself and watch him do the same as the woman continues to stare. What the actual fuck?

She looks down at me, large brown eyes in a pale face with a halo of golden hair waving down her back, and she smiles. "I'm his fiancée. Who are you?"

Sebastian practically growls at her. "What are you doing here, Celene?"

Celene. The bitch has a name.

She holds up a bag she's carrying. "I was going through some boxes in my garage and found a few things that belong to you. I thought you'd want them back. I knocked, but you didn't answer."

I climb out of the pool, tired of looking up at the asshole. "So you thought breaking and entering was a good plan?" I ask her. I know I should probably let Sebastian handle this, but I don't give a shit. Someone has some explaining to do, and since I still like the guy I'm fucking and I don't like this woman at all, I'm going to assume she's not supposed to be here until Sebastian corrects me.

She's taller than me, I realize, once I'm standing next to her. It irks me, and I'm not usually self-conscious about my height.

She doesn't look at me or acknowledge my words. Instead, she looks at Sebastian, who has come to stand beside me. "You didn't answer. I heard you back here and didn't think it would be a problem to poke my head in and drop this off. You're usually alone this time of night."

How the fuck does she know what he's doing in the middle of the night? And why would she choose this time to come by with his stuff?

"You don't live here anymore," he tells her. "You can't just come in when you feel like it. If you have something for me, call first."

Her face falls for just a moment. "I tried calling. You didn't pick up."

I raise my eyebrow at her. "Maybe that should have been a hint," I tell her.

She finally looks at me, her face returning to a scowl. "This doesn't concern you."

I laugh at that. A full on, out loud belly laugh. This throws her off her game a bit, but I can see Sebastian smiling from the corner of my eye. "I love how you're really trying to play this like you have any rights here. I'm a guest of Sebastian, in his house. We were enjoying a private moment in his backyard. I'm assuming, given your air of entitlement, that you're his *former* fiancée. That means you have no claim on him anymore. Or this house. You're trespassing, and that's a crime. And since I'm technically Sebastian's wife, all of this most definitely concerns me."

If I had a camera on me right now, I would take a picture of her, because that face is priceless. She stutters and stalls for a moment before blurting out, "Wife? He married...*you*?"

Her tone is insulting, but I expected nothing less, and I let it wash over me. Before I can respond though, Sebastian grabs her by the arm. "You need to leave. Don't come here again. This isn't your home anymore."

I go into the house to find something to wear while he escorts her back to her car. I don't like leaving them alone together, but I'm not going to traipse around naked or with a wet towel, either.

By the time Sebastian returns, I'm wearing one of his old t-shirts and a pair of his boxer shorts. "I hope you don't mind. I wasn't planning for an overnighter when I went out with Vi. If, that is, you still want me to stay overnight."

A part of me feels bad for using the wife card, since I don't plan on staying married to this man. But I can't stand Celene, and I knew those words would cut her deep. I don't feel bad about that part.

Sebastian drops his wet towel and walks over to me naked. He kisses me, pressing me against his now hard cock. "Yes, I want you to stay. I just want you, Kacie."

I want to ask him more about Celene, about their relationship, but I forget all my questions as he pulls up the shirt I'm wearing and bends down to take one of my nipples into his mouth.

Talking can happen later, I decide, as I give myself over to him yet again.

SIXTEEN

Breakfast and Boxers

I wake in the middle of the night to the sound of something beautiful filling my dreams. It's coming from downstairs, so I pull the sheet off the bed and wrap myself in it, then follow the music.

I find Sebastian sitting at the piano, lost in a sad song he's pouring into the instrument. His eyes are closed, and I think I detect a tear on his cheek. I pause, feeling like I'm intruding on something deeply personal, something he doesn't let very many people see.

I should go back upstairs, should give him his space, but I'm rooted to the ground, held captive by the bittersweet tenderness of his music.

When the last note drifts through the night, he looks up, startled to see me there.

"I'm sorry," I say. "I heard something and…"

"Come here, Kacie."

I walk toward him, and he pulls me into his arms, pressing me against the keys. "I'm glad you're here."

I rest my hands on the top of his head as he leans against my stomach, holding me. "Did you write that song?"

"Yes," he says. "For my child. It was the last song I played on this piano."

My heart leaps. "Child?"

He sits back and looks up at me. "Celene was my fiancée, as you've surmised. We got engaged when she found out she was pregnant. It was a happy time for us both. We bought this house with the intention of filling it with our children, our family. But six months into the pregnancy, she miscarried. It was just before Christmas, and they couldn't schedule the D&E until after the holiday. She had to carry our dead child through Christmas. After…after, things changed. We grew apart. We handled our grief differently and couldn't find a way to come together again after that. It was a few months later that I found out she was cheating on me with my best friend. We ended things then, once and for all."

I feel a twinge of grief for Celene, until I find out she cheated on Sebastian. He lost not only his child, but also the woman he loved. My heart swells with sadness for the man sitting before me. "I'm so sorry."

"It was a girl. We named her Hope." I feel his fingers dig into my back, his muscles flexing in remembered pain. "I blame myself. I'm a pediatric heart surgeon. My job is to save the lives of the children who can't be saved. And I couldn't save my own daughter."

There are no words that can bring him comfort right now, so instead I hold him and feel the warmth of his tears as he grieves.

...

The next morning the smell of coffee and bacon wakes me, and my stomach growls as I roll out of the now-empty bed and plod to the bathroom to freshen up.

When I come downstairs, now wearing my own clothes from the night before, I see Sebastian in the kitchen, wearing nothing but boxers, cooking.

The kitchen is filled with light from large windows, and his tanned skin is warm as I place a hand on his back. I just want to feel him. The brightness of the morning seems to push away any lingering darkness from last night.

He turns to me, smiling, all shadows gone from his eyes as he kisses me deeply, before directing his focus back to breakfast. He has two pans going, one with bacon and one with omelets filled with peppers and onions and cheese. My stomach grumbles again, and he laughs. "Hungry?"

"Last night did work up an appetite," I admit, helping myself to a cup of coffee. I inhale the scent before adding sugar and cream, then sit on a barstool and watch him cook. "I'd offer to help, but you look really sexy doing this all by yourself. I don't want to ruin the experience."

He puts a plate in front of me and piles bacon and an omelet onto it. "I wouldn't let you anyways. I enjoy cooking, especially for a beautiful woman."

Every time he calls me beautiful, my heart does a happy dance. I'm absurd, I know.

He takes a seat next to me, and we eat in silence for a moment. The breakfast is perfect, and I finish the plate, not even a little bit self-conscious of eating so much in front of him. Fuck that, I worked off this and more last night in bed and in the pool. The memory makes me smile, until I get to the part where the Wicked Witch of Las Vegas interrupted us. Maybe I should feel more kindly about her, given what I learned last night, but she's still a bitch.

"We know very little about each other," I tell him as I sip my coffee.

He looks at me, his eyes clear and beautiful. "There are many kinds of knowing, Kacie. There's the knowledge of random facts. I'll admit that we're short on those, but that's actually the easiest kind of knowledge to come by. Consider how much most Americans know about popular celebrities, without really knowing them at all. But there's also another kind of knowing. A recognition of the heart. That's what we have. My heart knows you. Your heart knows me. This summer is just a chance to get our minds caught up."

He places a hand on my thigh, caressing me. "And obviously our bodies are quite intimate with each other already."

His words stir something deep in me, but I shut it down, not ready to examine those feelings too closely. "Do you want to have a family? Children?"

His hand falls away, and I miss the warmth, but I don't say anything, waiting for him to answer me.

"I don't know. I'm scared to feel that kind of loss again. When Hope died, a part of me died too. And every day I'm reminded of her death as I try to save children too sick to walk, children with horrible illnesses who often don't make it. I don't know if I can go through that again with my own child."

I'm not sure how I feel about that. I haven't decided if I ever want kids, though I always assumed I'd have a few eventually. But do I really want them, or do I just think that because it's still the expected trajectory for a woman's life in our society? I haven't figured that out.

He stands and takes our plates to the sink to wash.

"Do you ever miss Celene?" I'm not sure I want to know the answer to this, but I ask it anyways.

"It was a long time ago. That relationship is dead and buried."

"It didn't seem very dead last night. At least not for her." I go to him, taking a hand towel from the counter, and dry as he washes. It's so domestic and feels so right.

"That may be true, but it's definitely over for me." His voice is hard when he says that.

"What about you?" he asks as we take our coffee to the backyard to enjoy the sun. "Anyone serious? Besides me, of course." He grins, and I melt a little.

"I had a boyfriend in college," I say. "It didn't go very far. I broke up with him before it could. Since then I've kept it casual. Tate and I knew we were meant for a life elsewhere. Out of Ohio. And even in college and grad school, I knew I wouldn't stay in those areas after graduation, and I didn't want the hassle of falling in love and having to negotiate where we would live. We knew we'd come to Las Vegas, as unorthodox as that choice was. Staying single made all of that easier."

He nods as if he understands, but I wonder if he really does. Men have long believed they could do anything, be anything, live anywhere, whereas women are often expected to sacrifice for their families, their husbands, their children. Men have a freedom of thought, a freedom of expectation to life that women have never had. Women have to constantly negotiate—with themselves, with others—for a semblance of those choices, those inalienable rights that men take for granted.

My phone beeps, distracting me from my thoughts. I pull it out of my pocket and check it, then smile and reply. Sebastian waits patiently until I'm done. "Anyone I should be jealous of?" he asks, teasing.

"Nope, just my brother. We have a date to jog this morning, so I have to get going. Are you working today?" I stand, finishing off my coffee and setting in on the table between us.

"I'm checking on some patients later. But I'd like to see you tonight. I have an idea to aid in us getting to know each other better. To put your mind at ease. I'll text you later with instructions."

I lift an eyebrow. "Instructions?"

He grins, then kisses me. "Trust me, you'll enjoy it."

He leaves to get dressed and drive me home, and I wander his house while I wait, my mind cataloging each of his belongings and wondering how many Celene picked out. The thoughts do not make me happy.

On the drive home, I ask him about his music. "Where did you learn to play the piano?"

"My parents insisted on piano lessons once I was old enough to reach the keys. I resisted for a long time, but then fell in love with music and drove them nuts, practicing day and night. At one point, I actually considered Julliard over medical school, but I knew I couldn't give up my dream of savings lives. "

It's not the answer I expected, and my heart softens even more to this amazing man next to me. Spending time with him so far has not helped in my plan to get sick of him, I realize. It's still early, though. Surely he has more faults that will eventually tip the scale and make it easier to let go.

But as I look at him, at his strong profile and his talented hands, as I reflect on the kind of person I've seen him to be thus far, my confidence waivers, and I worry I've gotten myself into something I may not be able to get out of without breaking both of our hearts.

SEVENTEEN
Running

"It's fucking hot," I say as Tate and I take another hill, our feet pounding the pavement in a familiar rhythm.

"If someone had come home last night, we could have gone running earlier, when it was cooler," he teases, nudging me in the shoulder.

Running isn't my favorite thing in the world to do, but it keeps me in shape when I can't get to a pool to do laps. Thinking of pools draws my thoughts back to last night, to Sebastian and his cock and fucking him in the cool water and the feel of his hands.

Now I'm even hotter. Great.

"Looks like you and lover-boy are getting serious," Tate says, probing for more.

"I told you, it's just a summer thing. I'm still filing the annulment papers first thing Monday morning."

He snickers. "I'm sure that's true, at least the filing part. The 'just a summer thing' part? Not so much. I've never seen you like this, sis. It's not just a fling."

The light ahead of us turns red, and we stop. I bend over, breathing hard, and take a swig of my water. Sweat is dripping down my face, stinging my eyes. I wipe it away and stretch, thinking about Tate's words. "You know I'm not going to get serious with him. And you know why. Now can we please change the subject?"

He rolls his eyes but doesn't push. "Fine, what do you want to talk about?"

I'm about to bring up our schedule for the next few weeks when he stops me with a look. "Except work. Anything but work."

We start running again. "Okay, what's going on with you and the girl from the bar. What was her name?"

"Stephanie," he says. "I'm not seeing her anymore. It didn't work out."

This time I snicker. "Let me guess. It didn't work out because you slipped, and your dick fell into someone else's vagina?"

He clasps a hand over his heart dramatically. "You wound me, sister, to think so little of me."

"So you didn't fuck someone else?"

"Well, I wouldn't say that. But I broke up with Stephanie before the actual penetration occurred. I'm not a total sleaze."

"Right. Bummer really, she seemed...nice."

He laughs. "Are you judging her by her choice of men or her attire, since you never actually spoke to her."

"I could go Mom on you and ask when you're going to settle down with a nice girl and have babies."

He swats at me, then runs ahead to avoid payback. "Hey, I could throw that right back at ya. Speaking of, Mom called last night while you were with Romeo. She wanted to talk to both of us together."

That's news. She hasn't called in a while. "What did you tell her?"

"That you were out fucking your new husband and wouldn't be home all night."

I nearly choke on another sip of water. "You didn't."

"No, I didn't. I told her you were out with Vi, and I wasn't sure when you'd be home."

"You'd better not tell them shit about this mess I'm in. They would freak."

A car swerves onto the sidewalk, nearly hitting us. I jump to the side and narrowly avoid the bumper. "Watch where you're going, asswipe."

"With such a lady-like demeanor, I'm honestly shocked you don't have more suitors," Tate teases, but I punch him, my heart still thumping in my chest from the near-collision.

"What did mom want?" I ask when I'm recovered enough to keep running. We're on the route back to our house, and my legs and ribs are burning, my lungs are dying, and I need a bath and a cold drink. God, I hate running sometimes.

"She said Grandma Gladys isn't doing well. She's back in the hospital. She wants us to come visit."

I make a very unladylike sound. "I'm not going back to Ohio just so that old nag can berate me for my life choices. Remember how she threatened to remove us from her will if we didn't move back to the country and do the whole family and kids thing?"

Tate nods. "Yeah, I remember. She was always a mean bitch. I can still feel the snap of the belt from her spankings when we were kids, and mom and dad forced us to spend a week of each summer with her."

"Where's social services when you need them?" I ask as we jog into our house, and I collapse into a sweaty mess on the couch. "So what did you tell mom?"

"That we are booked all summer, and we'll try to get out there, but no promises."

I nod in approval. "That should keep her off our backs for a while."

Tate presses the button on our answering machine to play the messages and then ambles into the kitchen and grabs two beers, tossing me one. I can't stand beer usually, but after a run, it's possibly the best thing in the world.

The first message is a telemarketer. I'd delete it, but I don't want to move that far, so we both just listen to the woman blabber on about the price of car insurance. The next message has me sitting up, hands clutching the couch anxiously.

"Ms. Michaels, this is David Melton's assistant. I'm calling to let you know that we received your gift basket and considered your ideas carefully. Mr. Melton was impressed and has asked that Hitched be put on the short list of companies we're considering for his bachelor party. We'll be in touch either way to let you know, but Mr. Melton was very excited by your proposal."

I'm clutching a throw pillow so hard it's about to burst, and once the message ends, I scream into it then jump up and start dancing around the house like a maniac. "I told you!" I tell Tate. "I told you my idea would work. We're a shoe-in!"

Tate smiles at me. "It's good news, but it's not a done deal. Don't count the chickens before they hatch."

"Okay, Mom. Look, he wouldn't have called us like that if it wasn't basically decided. Who else in town can provide what we're suggesting? I just know it's going to be us. Hitched is about to be famous!"

I'm still dancing around with my throw pillow, unwilling to let Tate's negative attitude pull me down, when the doorbell rings. Tate rolls his eyes and gets up to get the door, since I'm clearly not going to.

"Hey sis, I think it's for you." He comes back into the living room carrying a white box with a red ribbon.

I grin like the fool I am as he hands it to me, my energy climbing even higher. I eagerly open it, knowing it's from Sebastian.

Inside are some very sexy lingerie and a card.

A car will arrive to pick you up at 9 p.m.
Wear this under your clothes.
Bring an overnight bag.
Looking forward to "getting to know you better" tonight, Ms. Michaels.

Forever Yours,
Sebastian

EIGHTEEN
A Leap of Faith

I won't lie. Keeping my mind on work today has been hard. But I'm at least trying. Give me some credit, will ya?

Right now I'm with Vi, walking into the main office of Class A Skydiving, a local business that will hopefully be just what I need for my client, Joey. Because renting a tank didn't work out, at least not in Las Vegas. He took the news well and is now excited to jump out of airplanes. Men are easy.

I introduce myself to the receptionist, who buzzes the boss. When Carl Danton comes out, Vi raises an appreciative eyebrow at him, and I smile warmly. "I'm Kacie Michaels from Hitched. We spoke on the phone about doing a group skydiving for a party I'm planning. This is my associate, Vi Reynolds."

He shakes my hand and gives me a once over that I recognize. In the past his appraisal might have pulled some flirting out of me, but it seems my mind and body are Team Sebastian. I sigh mentally and get down to business.

"Let me give you ladies a tour of our place. We offer more than just skydiving. We have hot air balloons, exotic cars and helicopters. And we're more than happy to work with you on group events and rates."

I take in everything as he shows us their selection of cars, from Porsches to Lamborghinis to anything else you can imagine. A few helicopters are parked under the hanger, and everywhere people are bustling about, doing their job.

Mr. Danton is telling us about his safety measures when my phone buzzes. I pull it out and check my text, blushing as I read it.

Please tell me you're missing my cock as much as I'm missing your pussy.

What timing Dr. Donovan has. I glance at Vi, who, I can tell, knows exactly what's going on, then I bow my head and reply quickly.

You're interrupting a business meeting with all this naughtiness. And now my panties are wet, and my nipples are about to pop out of my blouse. I want you inside me. See you soon. And thank you for the gift.

It's hard to focus the rest of the tour, but I take notes, negotiate a price for their party and leave happy in the knowledge that we'll be able to provide our clients with what they want. I also realize that this company has just solved my problem of how to live up to my promises for the Melton party. I'm feeling giddy as everything starts to line up perfectly.

As Vi pulls out of the parking lot, my phone buzzes again.

Karpov Kinrade

I'm imagining the way your pussy tastes on my tongue as I eat you until you come on my face. I want you to scream for me, Kacie.

I giggle. Yes, giggle. And reply, as Vi rolls her eyes.

Mmm can't wait. I suppose you'll want me to suck on your cock again as well. I'll try to suck deeper this time, taking you all the way into my throat until you explode in my mouth.

"I take it things are going well with the doctor?" Vi asks, and I can tell this is going to be near identical to my conversation with Tate.

To avoid that, I ask about Chad. "Is he moving in?"

"I gave him a drawer and space for his toothbrush. We'll see how it goes from there."

"Does he mind what you do for a living?" I've always wondered how she balances a personal relationship while also acting as Dom for men who get off on being her submissive.

"No. He knows that for me it's not sexual. That's enough for him, I think." She almost sounds disappointed, which doesn't really make any sense. She loves her work, so I would think she'd be happy to find someone who's comfortable with it.

"Anything else going on?" I ask.

"Nothing really. Just thinking about my future and trying to make some decisions about what I really want out of my life." The melancholy in her voice deepens, and I know something more is going on.

"That's what you call 'nothing'? What gives, Vi? Are you unhappy?"

She shakes her head. "Not the way I was when I was a bank manager. That job nearly killed my soul. I guess I'm just wondering if this is it? If this is everything for me, or if there's something more that I'm not seeing?"

"I suppose we all wonder that," I say. Though it's been a long time since I've done serious soul searching about my path in life. I've known what I want for a long time, and I've gone after it with pit bull focus and determination. Same with Tate. We never questioned it. We just knew.

But meeting Sebastian has opened a door in me I don't want to walk through. I know there are questions behind that door that won't be so clear cut and easy to answer, and I'm not ready for that much introspection.

"What are you going to do?" I ask.

She shrugs. "Probably nothing. You know how I get. It'll pass after a while. I have a great life. I don't want to upset the apple cart just because I'm having a few off days."

"If you need anything..." I let my voice trail off, knowing she knows I'm here for her.

She reaches over and squeezes my hand. "I know. Thank you. You and Tate are my family. I'd be lost without you."

When we get to my house, she doesn't come in. "I have a client in a few hours and a date with Chad later. But have fun tonight."

"Thanks for coming with me," I hold the door to her car as I stand on the sidewalk. "It was fun hanging with you a bit."

She smiles. "We should go skydiving sometime. That owner is hot."

"I'll pass, thanks. Heights and me aren't BFFs. Plus, we're both dating people right now."

She laughs. "That doesn't mean we can't look—and admire!"

I close the door and roll my eyes at her as she speeds away.

When I walk into the house, there's a new bouquet of roses on my desk with a note from Sebastian.

I miss how you feel. See you soon.

The card smells like him. A spicy, woody scent with hints of cardamom and cinnamon. I take the card up to my room, smiling all the way, as I dress for my date with the sexiest man alive.

NINETEEN
Getting to Know You

He knows me well. The lingerie fits perfectly, and I feel very sexy as I slip into the limousine he hired to pick me up.

The driver offers me champagne, which I accept, and I sip it as he drives me to Sebastian's house. I realize once again I'll need a ride from him to get home tomorrow, but I don't mind a bit.

I've got my overnight bag, and as I step out of the limo, I worry I'll be overdressed for what he has planned. I'm wearing one of my more formal gowns, a long black dress with rhinestones on my breasts and at the hem that twinkle like diamond stars.

My hair is pulled into an up-do, and my makeup is more dramatic than usual.

But when Sebastian comes out of the house, he's dressed in a tux, and I release the breath I've been holding, happy that we coordinated so well tonight.

I still have no idea what he's planning, but I'm on fire with anticipation.

He takes my bag from me, slips the driver some money, and leads me through the front walkway of glowing orbs and into his house.

I gasp.

The entire living room and up the stairway: everything is covered in flickering candles. It's stunning. Add to that, white Christmas lights have been strategically placed to give the entire house a fairytale vibe. On a table in the living room lay a spread of desserts, fruits, champagne and wine, and finger foods that make my mouth water. It's enough food for a party, but we are the only ones in attendance.

The fire is burning bright in the stone fireplace, and the light from the flames dance over the walls. In front of the fire is an extra thick fur rug I didn't see before, piled with large pillows and a few soft blankets. There's another smaller table there with two glasses of champagne and a bowl of fresh strawberries and cream.

Sebastian stands with his hand on my lower back, silent as I take in the room. "You did all this for me?"

He kisses my head. "Anything for you."

He puts my bag on the couch and offers me the champagne, which I take, sipping on it. "So, the plan tonight is to eat until we both have to be rolled out of the house?"

"The plan is to get to know each other. Creatively."

I follow his eyes to something I didn't notice before. Two stacks of playing cards, but not the normal kind. "What's this?"

"Our game for the night."

We sink into the pillows, and I pluck a strawberry out of the bowl and dip it into whipped cream. "Do you have more of this? It could come in handy."

"Oh it will." He smiles seductively as I lick the cream off the fruit.

As I finish the strawberry, he leans into me, licking a bit of cream off my lower lip as he kisses me. "You taste sweet," he says.

"I *am* sweet," I say, smiling with fake demureness.

"Which is why you're going to be *my* dessert." He smiles wickedly. "Later."

I inhale sharply, his delicious scent playing with my nose as I imagine his tongue doing delicious things to my body.

He picks up two dice and hands them to me. "First, we role to see who goes first in our little game. Ladies first."

I roll an eight. He takes the dice and clicks them around in his hand, then lets them go. Ten.

"You cheated," I say, smiling.

"You caught me," he says, raising his arms in the air. "I'm a professional poker shark. These are weighted."

"So, how does this game work?"

His eyes glint mischievously as he holds the deck out to me. "Draw a card and ask me the question on it. If I answer incorrectly, I have to draw a card from this deck," he points to the other set of cards still lying on the rug, "and do what the card says to do. If *you* answer incorrectly, you have to draw a card and do what it says. And if one of us answers correctly, the other person draws a card and follows the instructions."

"Sounds simple enough. What kind of questions are these?" I ask as I draw the first card.

"Personal ones," he says.

I look down at my hand and smile. There's no way he's going to get this answer correct. "What was the name of my first grade teacher?"

He exaggerates a thinking expression, finger tapping his jaw and then snaps his fingers. "Mrs. Brandy. And you once said your dad likes brandy, and the whole class laughed, and your teacher turned red and gave you time out."

My jaw drops. "How the fuck do you know that?"

"I have my ways. Draw a card, my dear."

I do and read what it says. "Kiss your partner anywhere on their body for three seconds."

He holds his arms out wide. "I'm all yours. Pick a spot, darling."

I roll my eyes at him and then grab his hand, planting my lips on it to the count of three. "Done. Your turn."

He looks at his hand and frowns. "I think you need help understanding the point of this game." He picks a card and reads his question. "What's my favorite color?"

His cobalt blue eyes are laughing at me. Damn this man. I mentally review the clothes I've seen him in, the decor of his house and anything else I can remember from the times I've spent with him while not drunk. "Red," I guess.

He smiles. "That's correct. What gave me away?"

"Your ties," I tell him, holding out the naughty deck, as I'm now calling it. "They all have bold splashes of red in them."

"Good eye, darling. I guess I have to draw."

He reads the card silently before speaking. "Pick an exposed spot of skin on your partner's body and get creative."

He looks me over, his eyes hungry. My arms, parts of my legs, my neck, face...there are many parts for him to "get creative" with, and I wait, breath tight, as he decides what he's going to do and where he's going to do it.

Slowly he lifts my hand from my lap, exposing the inside of my wrist. First, his thumb caresses the soft skin, sending shivers through my body; then he brings it to his lips. I can feel his breath first, hot and enticing, then his lips brush against the thin blue veins under my pale skin. When his teeth graze that same spot, biting gently into flesh, I nearly come undone. He ends with a kiss and places my hand back into my lap. "A little taste of what's to come," he says, his voice deep.

I try to keep my cool, to pretend that his touch, his teeth, his kiss, didn't just light a fire inside me that will be impossible to extinguish, but I'm sure I fail miserably.

I draw the next card. "Where was I born?"

"Mansfield, Ohio," he says without a pause. How the hell does he know these things?

He sees the question in my eyes and laughs. "We shared a lot the night we married," he says. "I happen to remember it all."

And I don't. That puts me at a distinct disadvantage.

I pull a card since he got the answer correct. "Have your partner close their eyes and do something titillating to them."

He closes his eyes while I consider what "titillating" thing I should do. I decide to keep it simple. I lean in and first run a finger gently across his lower lip, then I bring my face closer to his, brushing my lips against his, teasing open his mouth with my tongue. I make the kiss delicate, sensuous, as tortuous as I can without giving him everything, while I run a fingernail lightly down his neck.

Our breath mingles, tongues barely touching as our lips continue to find brief moments of connection.

And then I pull away and lean back into my pillow. "Was that titillating enough?"

He opens his eyes and grins at me. "Oh yes. And I'll remember that when it's my turn."

A shiver of anticipation courses through me as he draws another card.

"Next question," he says. "Who's my favorite entertainer?"

I have no idea, because even though we both live in Las Vegas, we haven't talked about pop culture much.

"It's actually someone right here in Las Vegas," he says. "David Melton."

"The magician?" I ask, while trying a flaky cheese-filled treat.

He nods.

I grin widely. "He might become a client of Hitched."

His eyes widen. "Really? How?"

I explain about my gift basket and the call and end with my plans to take over the world.

"You're a genius," he says. "I used to watch his shows, and I've been to his live performance a few times. I haven't seen his latest one yet, but it's on my to-do list. I don't believe in magic, but he certainly has me wondering how he does it all without any help from the supernatural."

"I think it's magic," I say. "Real magic. Nothing else makes sense. Some of that stuff just can't be faked."

Sebastian laughs. "It can all be explained, somehow. No magic involved. Just science. Logic. Trickery."

"Remember that time he made that guy disappear and then reappear *in another country with his family!* That was crazy. No way could that be faked. There has to be some deals with the devil or voodoo or something going on." I've always been convinced that magicians of Melton's caliber have some kind of hidden power none of us have. It's too amazing to be otherwise. I know this makes me sound silly, but not everything in the world can be explained and rationalized.

Sebastian leans over and kisses me. "I believe in one kind of magic, and that's the magic of how you make me feel when we're together."

"You have a way with the words," I tell him.

"I want to have my way with you."

I pull out of his grasp. "Not until we finish our game."

He groans and sits back in his spot. "Have you seen Melton perform live?"

"No. Believe it or not, I haven't seen any shows on the Strip since moving here."

"Seriously?" He asks.

"Seriously. We've either been too busy or too broke. Or both. I want to though. Especially *Le Reve*. I hear it's beautiful."

"That's one I haven't seen either, but the reviews are terrific. Looks like we just found our next date night." He winks at me and draws another card.

Which, of course, I answer incorrectly. Again. And I have to strip. I choose my shoes—first, because my feet hurt, and second because I want to tease him before taking off anything too revealing. I quickly learn after a few more turns that while I don't suck at guessing things about him that are simple, I still can't remember more than fleeting glimpses of that night. I also learn that the purple cards will mean one of us has to take off some clothes.

I'm hoping I guess a few more questions correctly as I watch him strip his shirt off, his muscles ripped and oh-so-sexy. I guessed his favorite food—Italian. And for that I get a nice view of the abs. I feel very lucky right now.

My luck does not last though, and it isn't long before I find myself wearing only the lingerie he had delivered to me. I don't feign embarrassment; instead I sip at the champagne, my fourth glass, and bite into a piece of dark chocolate, nearly moaning with the pleasure at the bittersweet flavor.

"I like watching you eat," he says. "You make love to food with your mouth. Though I admit to being jealous. I'd like that mouth on me."

Before he can distract me with another kiss, I grab a card from the deck. The question makes me pause. "What's my greatest fear?"

I hold my breath wondering how well he really knows me. Not just the trivia, but also the real me.

"The night we met, you told me it was ants. Which I find amusing, I must admit."

I'm about to tell him he's wrong, with some outward gloat, but an inward sadness. Sometimes we all want to be seen. Truly seen, you know?

But before I can talk, he reaches for my hand. "I don't think that's true, though," he says softly. "I think your greatest fear is becoming invisible. Losing yourself, your life, to someone else's dreams or plans. I think your greatest fear is not fully realizing every potential you carry inside of yourself."

My breathing stops, and my eyes fill with unwanted tears. I curse them. And him. And everything.

He leans toward me. "I see you, Kacie Michaels. And I don't want to change you. I want to love you as the amazing woman you already are, and I want to witness what else you accomplish with all that spirit you have. I want to be a part of that, not thwart it."

The game is forgotten then. As is the food, and the whipped cream. I thought we would fuck tonight. I thought we would get naughty and eat things off each other's body and do all manner of illicit and erotic things to each other.

But what is happening now is more than that. It's more than fucking as he stares into my eyes and slowly peels off what's left of my clothes.

It's more than sex as he lowers his powerful body over mine.

It's more than mutual pleasure as he pushes his cock into me.

As we become one.

As our flesh joins together, our hearts locked in the same rhythm, breathing each other's breath.

As we make love for the first time.

TWENTY
Weekend Plans

For the next few weeks, Sebastian and I spend nearly every night together. As I slink into the house one morning after a particularly late night talking, laughing, watching our favorite movies, making love...Tate corners me in the kitchen as I add sugar to my coffee.

"The prodigal sister returns, and not in the clothes you were wearing last night. Did the good doctor give you a drawer?" he asks, looking around for my bags.

"Yes, actually. And a key to his house." Which I'd been reluctant to accept, but it made the most sense, since he lives alone and we spend most of our time at his house.

Tate pulls himself up and sits on the counter, watching me wipe up spilled sugar. "It's getting serious." He doesn't say it as a question, but as a statement. And with his grown-up voice, as if to emphasize the actual seriousness of the situation.

"It's a summer fling. What have you been up to?"

"Nope, that's not going to work this time. This isn't a fling, and you know it, and you need to be honest with this guy if you're really planning on breaking his heart at the end of the summer. He doesn't deserve that."

I push down a flare of anger at being lectured by my womanizing brother on how to treat people in a romantic relationship. "Says the guy who doesn't bother calling a girl the next day. Look, Sebastian knows how I feel. Why does everything have to be defined and decided on now? Can't we just enjoy getting to know each other without all the pressure? I'm sick of it."

I'm about to stalk out of the kitchen, when Tate hops off the counter and stops me. "You're right; I'm sorry. I'm not in a position to judge anyone. I just don't want *you* to get hurt."

I soften my scowl. "I'm fine."

I walk to my desk and flip through the messages Tate left. There's one that catches my eye. "Mom called again?"

"Yeah. I didn't want to bother you, but apparently our beloved grandmother is getting worse. Mom insists we come visit."

I raise an eyebrow. "Insists? And she'll do what if we don't?"

He shrugs. "I'm just passing the message along. We also got a few new client calls."

I sink into my leather desk chair and fire up my MacBook. "Let's focus on that and forget all the drama, shall we? I need to lose myself in work today."

He nods and takes a seat at his own desk. We spend the rest of the day working hard, making plans for several other parties we have booked and placing ads in newspapers locally and in California, since a lot of Californians use Vegas as their last minute wedding destination.

At the end of the day, Tate brings me another cup of coffee and sits on the edge of my desk. "Are you gone again tonight?"

I realize he looks lonely. "No, Sebastian has to work tonight. I'm all yours. What do you want to do?"

He smiles, his blue eyes brightening. "How about Chinese take-out and movies?"

"Sounds perfect," I say, returning his smile. "Shall I invite Vi? We haven't hung with her in a while."

He nods, pulling out his phone. "I'll order food, you order the dominatrix."

"Haha! But fine. Order extra orange chicken. She always hogs it."

An hour later, the three of us are stuffing our faces with the best Chinese in town and laughing at Channing Tatum as he grabs his partner's ball sack, thinking it's a grenade. Oh comedy—gotta love it.

After dinner, while Vi and Tate argue about the next movie choice and whether Adam Sandler or Channing Tatum is funnier (Channing always and forever, obviously, so in this I have to side with Vi), I liberate a few bottles of wine from our well-stocked cellar. I'm totally kidding here. We don't have a cellar, let alone a well-stocked one, but wouldn't it be cool to say that? No, I just pull the last two bottles of cabernet sauvignon out of our pantry, where they were stored next to our emergency macaroni and cheese boxes for nights when nothing else will fix life but mac and cheese from a box. Fortunately for my thighs, those nights don't happen often.

My phone buzzes while I pour three glasses. I check it, my pulse already accelerating in anticipation.

That brat. It's not Sebastian, as I'd obviously hoped, but rather Vi telling me to hurry up with the wine. "You're cruel," I holler from the kitchen as I cork the wine and balance three glasses.

"Oh, did you think it was from lover boy?" She bats her eyelashes and flips her long red hair dramatically.

"Fuck you," I say, handing her a glass.

"Thems is fighting words, but I'll forgive you now that I have this." She holds her glass up to her lips and sips. "Drink of the gods," she sighs.

Tate thanks me for his, smirking at our exchange, and I flop between the two of them. "Okay, what did you two decide for the next movie?"

They share a conspiratorial look and turn on the movie.

I laugh. "Gross Anatomy? Really? We're doing 80s movies now?"

Vi nudges me. "No, we're doing hot doctor movies now. We thought you might be in withdrawal, since it's been at least fifteen hours since you saw him last."

The sad thing is…I am. I miss him and am bummed he hasn't texted. But I'm not going to be that girl who can't go twenty-four hours without a guy. Nope. Not me.

My phone buzzes, and I jump to check it.

It's him.

My heart lifts, and I smile, knowing my twin and my best friend are mocking me. I don't care. Because apparently I *am* going to be that girl who acts like a crushing thirteen-year-old every time Sebastian texts me.

Missing me yet?

My fingers fly over the keypad.

Hadn't thought about you all day, actually. :P

His response comes quickly.

Pity. I've been thinking about you all day. And all the things I'm going to do to you when next we see each other.

My heart flip-flops.

And when might that be?

Ah, so you are *missing me, then?*

Maybe a little.

I have a proposition for you.

I pause for a moment before replying.

Does this involve another drunken wedding?

In a manner of speaking. My uncle is getting married at my parent's house in a few weeks. I was wondering if you would like to be my date. We'd be there from Friday to Sunday at the end of the month.

Wow. This is huge. Too huge. Meeting his whole family? Attending weddings together? We'd be like—I gulp—a couple.

Vi grabs the phone from me before I can react, and she reads the messages out loud. Then she types on my phone and clicks send. I pull the phone out of her hand.

"What have you done?"

She smirks at me. "Made things easier for you. You'll have a blast."

I look at my phone.

I'd love to. :) Sounds wonderful. When do we leave?

"Vi, I can't go to this wedding with him. It's the last thing I should be doing!"

"It'll be fun," she says.

Tate frowns. "We have a party that weekend."

I smile, vindicated. "See? Can't go."

Vi waves off my concern. "I've already mentally cleared my schedule. I got it covered."

Tate high fives her across my body, and I scowl at them both. "You suck."

"Go meet his family. It'll help you learn more about him and whether he's right for you or not," she says seriously.

I guess if the point of this summer is to get to know each other, then this is an important step. Realizing how little of his life outside of me I know about him, I decide tomorrow I will also drop in on him at work.

I can imagine nothing sexier than him in his scrubs, saving the lives of children.

TWENTY ONE
Grey's Anatomy

I know most people don't like hospitals, but I actually find them reassuring. I like knowing there are entire structures set up to help those who are sick or injured, and that these buildings are filled with people who are devoting their lives to saving people. That's pretty awesome, when you think about it.

When I arrive at Sunrise Children's Hospital, I admire its attempt at modern-looking architecture. Big windows, sharp angles, cement and glass and metal. I park and make my way to the front desk where they direct me to pediatrics. He doesn't know I'm coming, which may be a mistake. I start to regret my impulsive decision to bring him lunch.

I exit the elevator on his floor and am about to get back on, having chickened out, when someone calls my name.

I turn and see Dr. Donovan looking oh-so-sexy in khakis, a buttoned down shirt and a white doctor coat with a stethoscope around his neck. He smiles when I turn, his eyes bright and glued to me as he takes long strides to reach me.

Hitched

I wait, wondering what kind of greeting to expect while he's at work. He hugs me, then kisses me deeply as nurses gawk, and a few shoot me not-so-friendly glances. Guess he's popular.

"What are you doing here?" he asks.

I hold up the brown bag I'm carrying. "I brought you lunch." I shrug sheepishly and smile. "Surprise?"

"That's a wonderful surprise, and I actually have a few minutes. Let's go to my office."

Relief sinks into me as I follow him through the long white corridors. His office is neat and sparse, with the exception of the wall of medical books to the left of his desk.

I put the lunch on his desk, and he closes the door behind him.

"It's so good to see you," he says. "I was afraid I'd scared you off after inviting you to the wedding this month."

That's closer to the truth than he realizes, but I don't tell him that. I'm enjoying how happy he is to see me and don't want to ruin it. "I'm still here," I assure him, taking out the turkey sandwiches on rye I made, along with homemade pasta salad and a piece of pie for each of us.

Instead of sitting behind his desk, he takes the seat next to me, and we begin eating.

"How's your day going?" I ask.

He nods, wiping a bit of mustard off his lips. "Good. I have a patient, Shannon, she's six, and we've been worried about her for a while. We're waiting on a donor for her heart transplant, and she's been touch and go, but she's finally stabilizing and I'm confident she'll make it."

I take a sip of the soda I brought before speaking. "That's...so sad. I can't imagine what she and her parents must be going through. And to know that another child has to die to save her..."

"That's the hardest part of my job," he says.

"I couldn't do it. I couldn't have a job where life and death rested in my hands like that. It's amazing anyone can. You're a modern day hero," I tell him.

"I'm not the hero; those kids are."

My heart melts.

He picks up a napkin and brushes a crumb off my lip, then smiles. "How's your day going? Any new clients?"

"The schedule is looking good," I say, pleased that he's taking an interest in my work. "I'm still waiting to hear back about doing the party for Melton. That would make our career."

"I can't believe he called you. That's incredible. I'm so proud of you, either way."

"Technically, it was his assistant," I say. "But thanks. I'm pretty stoked. I have a good feeling about it."

We finish our sandwiches, and as I clear the trash off his desk, he comes up behind me and wraps his arms around my waist, pressing himself into me. "I'm really glad you came to surprise me today."

I twist in his arms to face him, my ass pressed against the edge of his desk. "I'm really glad I came too."

"I've missed the feel of you," he says, running his hand over my thigh as my skirt inches up higher.

"You're feeling me now," I remind him, my hands exploring his muscles.

"Not enough of you. I want to be inside of you. Do you want my cock inside of you, Kacie?" His hand slips between my legs, and he's rubbing my clit through my panties, so obviously my answer is a resounding yes.

With enthusiasm he pulls my panties down, and I kick them off. With my skirt now pushed to my waist, Sebastian unzips his own pants, spreads me and shoves his hard cock into me.

The sex is frantic, fast, intense as he frees my breasts and plays with them while pounding me. The carnal nature of this, in his office no less, makes me wet and desperate for more.

In this position, as my ass is pushed against the desk that I'm half sitting on, his pelvic bone rubs against my clit while he's fucking me, making my orgasm come quickly, deeply, shaking my whole body until I'm breathless. He holds me up, his arms around me, hands on my hips, as he keeps up the pace. His abs clench, muscles tensing as an orgasm rips through him.

He's moaning my name into my hair when the door behind us opens, and a woman speaks.

"Really, Sebastian? Is it bring-your-slut-to-work day?"

I'm too shocked to speak. As Sebastian pulls out of me and zips himself back up before turning to face what can only be his bitchy ex-fiancée, I find the presence of mind to close my legs, even if my panties are conspicuously on the floor in front of us.

When my brain finally starts working again, I wonder what the hell is she doing here?

Then I look at her closely. She's wearing a white jacket with a hospital ID. So she's a doctor.

Fuck me.

My stomach sinks to the floor, and I feel like I'm going to be sick. He still works with her? He sees her everyday? And he didn't mention this to me?

"You might try knocking," he growls at her. "This isn't your office."

"I didn't realize I'd be walking in on a sex show," she says, clearly not sorry.

"It's not your business. And you owe my *wife* an apology."

She looks aghast. I'm guessing she's done her best to put our nuptials out of her mind. "I refuse to apologize to your sex toy. You and I both know this is nothing but a drunken mistake that won't last. You deserve better than the likes of her."

I'm about to push myself past Sebastian and bitch-slap her, when he pulls me against him. "Get out, Celene."

She tosses a file on the desk next to where my naked ass just was. "That's the file you wanted on Shannon. You're welcome."

She storms out, and I'm still shaking.

Sebastian looks at me, his face in a frown. "I'm so sorry. She had no right to speak to you that way."

"Why didn't you tell me she works here with you?"

I pull out of his grasp and grab my underwear, slipping them on under my skirt.

"It's not important. She's not important. We're just colleagues. Nothing more."

I nod, but I'm hurt and not ready to deal with this right now. "I have to go, and you probably have work to do."

Hitched

I'm at the door when he catches my hand. "I'm truly sorry. Please forgive me."

"There's nothing to forgive." I let him kiss me, then I leave.

I'm nearly out of the hospital, and I'm doing a damn good job holding in all the emotions flooding me, when the bitch sees me and walks briskly over to me. I can keep walking, but she'll probably use her demon powers to catch me.

Instead, I stop, waiting for her, mildly curious as to what she might have to say.

Her first words surprise me.

"I'm sorry. What I said was uncalled for. It's hard seeing him with someone else."

I almost feel sorry for her, until I remember why they're not together anymore. "I'm sure that's how he felt when you cheated on him."

She flinches. "You're right. It probably is. Look, I don't know you, and you're probably a really great person. Maybe we could even have been friends under different circumstances."

Yeah, no.

"But I wasn't entirely wrong in what I said. This," she gestures to the hospital around her, "is his life. He lives and breathes his vocation. His calling as a doctor. He needs someone who understands this part of him. Who lives it too. Can you give him that? Can you be who he really needs for the rest of his life?"

She doesn't wait for an answer, and I have none to give her as I walk to my car, a lonely hole growing inside of me.

I open my car door, ready to sulk away, nursing my heartache in silent martyrdom, when Sebastian calls my name.

He's running toward me, briefcase in hand. "Wait, please!"

I stand by the door, surprised to see him. "Aren't you supposed to be working?" I ask.

"My work is done for the day. I left the reports until the morning. I couldn't let you leave alone after that." He reaches for my hand and holds it in his. "I'm sorry. I should have told you about working with Celene. You have every right to be hurt. Can you forgive me?"

Damn it. I can't stay mad at this man. "Yes, of course. I just really hate that bitch."

He laughs. "Yes, well…But let's not let her get in the way of us. Okay?"

I step closer to him. "Are you really taking the rest of the day off?"

He nods, slipping an arm around me. "If you'll spend it with me."

TWENTY TWO
Unexpected Phone Call

The last week with Sebastian has been a whirlwind of romance. I know this isn't what real relationships are like all the time, but I cherish the moments while they last, knowing at the very least we are creating memories I can savor for a lifetime, regardless of where we end up when fall comes.

Right now, I'm enjoying a foot massage by the skilled doctor as we watch re-runs of old sitcoms and drink wine. His fingers are strong, and he knows just where to put pressure at the base of my feet. I smile at him as I take another sip of my drink. "If life as a world-class pediatric heart surgeon no longer satisfies, you could always make a living as a masseuse."

He smiles back at me, his eyes happy and face so beautiful it makes me breathless. "Thanks, but I'm good. You, however, are welcome to these hands whenever you want."

He tucks my feet to the side and leans his body over mine until we are face to face, our bodies draped over the couch. In the background, a soundtrack offers canned laughs as the main character says something self-deprecating and funny. I ignore them and focus on the man in front of me.

"I like having exclusive access to those hands," I say.

Propping himself on one arm, he uses his free hand to unbutton the pajama top I'm wearing. "And I like having access to these." His hand slides over one breast, then the other, my nipples hardening at his touch, skin shivering with desire.

My phone rings on the table in front of the couch, but I ignore it. It's Tate's ring tone. I'll call him back. After.

It goes silent for a moment as Sebastian brings his mouth to my nipple and sucks.

I arch my back.

My cell phone rings again. Tate. Again.

A twinge of worry forms in the back of my mind, but I push it aside.

When he calls again, I sigh and reach for my phone. "He wouldn't be calling this often if there wasn't something wrong," I say by way of apology for throwing cold water on our sexy times.

"This better be good," I say, answering the phone.

"Kacie, I just got a call from Mom."

My heart speeds up at the sound of Tate's voice. Sad, stressed. "What's wrong?"

"Our grandmother died this morning. The funeral is scheduled for this weekend. We have to go back to Ohio, sis."

I tell him I'll be home shortly and put my phone down. Sebastian frowns, concern written on his face, and sits up. I button up my shirt before telling him what happened. "I have to go. Tate and I will need to make plans to fly home for the funeral."

It all feels distant. Unreal. There's no love lost between me and my grandmother, but still, the thought that she's dead, and that I'll have to go back to my old home, my old life…it all feels…surreal.

Sebastian pulls me into a hug, but if he's expecting tears, he'll be disappointed. I have none in me.

"I can change a few things in my schedule and come with you," he says.

I adore him more than anything in that moment, but I say no. "Tate will be with me. And we weren't close to her. I'll just be gone a few days. Thank you, though, for the offer. I can't tell you what that means, knowing you'd drop everything to be there for me."

He strokes the side of my face with his hand, then kisses my forehead. "I'm always here for you."

It only takes me a few minutes to pack up my bag and change out of my pajamas. He walks me to my car, and we kiss again. I rest my hands on his chest, memorizing his face, sad that our weekend plans will have to wait. "I'll call you and let you know when I get there and where I'm staying."

"I'll be waiting for your call."

TWENTY THREE

Blast from the Past

Tate and I say little during our hour-long drive from the airport in Cleveland to Mansfield. He offers to drive the rental, and I don't argue. I wonder how my mother is handling the death of her own mother. As much as I don't want to be home again, I also want to support my mom during what must be a painful time for her.

As we drive, I admire the beauty of Ohio. I couldn't wait to leave this place, but coming back, I have to admit that it has charm. Lush green, even in summer, and there are pastures and trees as far as the eye can see. It's so different from the concrete jungle of Las Vegas, and it brings up childhood memories of building forts and swimming in the lake near our house and cheering for our high school football team on crisp autumn nights.

We are nearly home, and Tate points out our old high school. I can see the stadium and remember my first kiss under those bleachers with Bradley Davis, the quarterback. Tate punched him in the face the next day when Bradley told everyone in the boy's locker room that he'd felt me up.

He hadn't.

After that, no one dared spread rumors about me, but it was a bit harder to get a date. Tate had that effect on potential male suitors.

Ah, memory lane.

"Do you think any of our old teachers still work there?" Tate asks as the school fades from view.

"Probably Mr. Schraeder. I don't think he'll ever retire his reign of terror on the children of Mansfield."

Tate chuckles. "Remember when his bald head turned red yelling at you for leaving class to pee? I thought he'd rupture an artery."

"I certainly hoped he would. It was so stupid. I was done with my test and had turned it in. It wasn't like I could cheat. And I was going to pee, one way or another. I just didn't want to do it on the floor in the classroom."

He turns right, and the houses look familiar. We're close. My palms are slick with sweat.

"I can't believe Mom grounded you for that," he says, frowning.

"Oh, you know our parents. Sticklers for the rules and respect. Heaven forbid a girl is in the right when a male teacher is wrong."

My phone beeps, and I check it, smiling.

Made it safe, I hope? Missing you.

Sebastian. My heart hurts at how much I already miss him.

Missing you too. Just getting to my parents house. Funeral is tomorrow at 2. We should be coming home Sunday.

Not sure I'll make it that long, but I'll try. Would it be inappropriate to say that I miss the feel of being inside of you?

A buzz of remembered pleasure courses through me.

Thanks for making me hot and bothered right before seeing my family for the first time in forever. I owe you for that.

If payment includes you being in my arms, I'll gladly accept it.

We pull into my parents' driveway, and I take a deep breath and get out, stuffing my phone into my pocket.

It's the smell that hits me first. Too many flowers and the scent of casseroles. It smells like a funeral.

And it looks like old school country with floral everything and knick-knacks everywhere.

My mom comes out of the kitchen wearing an apron, her eyes red-rimmed but nothing else out of place. Her brown hair has faded, leaving more strands of grey than I remember seeing last time, and there are new lines on her face. I realize with shock that my mother is getting old. She smiles when she sees us. "My two long-lost prodigal children home at last."

"Hi Mom." I reach over to give her a hug. "How you holding up?"

She brushes aside my concern. "I'm fine of course. Your grandmother has been sick a long time. We knew it was coming. I just wish you could have come before she died. She would have liked to see you in the end."

I don't know how to reply to that so I don't say anything. Tate saves us from the awkward silence by offering his own hug and then rubbing his stomach. "It smells delicious in here. Any chance some of that food is for me?"

I roll my eyes at him when my mother turns away to lead us into the kitchen, but I follow, because I too could use something to eat.

"Where's Dad?" I ask, looking around. The kitchen hasn't changed at all. The red teapot is still on the same stove, with cast iron pots hanging over the island. The same maple oak table sits to the side, by the window, and I have a flash of sitting there with Tate and our sister Jessica, eating freshly baked cookies and drinking milk. I smile at the memory as we each sit where we always sat as a family, while my mother serves us lunch.

"He's around here somewhere," she says.

As if on cue, my dad comes in. He's a big man with a lot of meat on his bones, though not fat. He fills a room with his presence, and when he sees us, he grins. "Why didn't you tell me you were here!"

He kisses the top of my head, shakes Tate's hand and sits down next to us, waiting for his lunch.

My mom joins us last with her own plate. It's a casserole, of course, but it's good, and I have second.

They ask about our business and our lives. We keep our answers brief because they don't really want to know the details of what we do.

"And what about any men in your life, Kacie? I'd love some grandchildren before I'm too old to enjoy them, assuming you'd ever bring them to visit." My mom tries to say this lightly, but it comes out bitter.

"Why do you never ask Tate these questions? He's the same age as me and just as capable of making babies."

My mom collects our dirty dishes and begins washing them and putting them away. "Don't start, Kacie. We don't need your feminist nonsense this weekend. I just want to see you settled down and happy before it's my funeral you're all attending."

Dad looks away, clearly uncomfortable with all this "female emotion" as he always called it. Finally, he clears his throat. "Well, I'd best be getting back to work. Need to mow the lawn and clean up the yard a bit before the funeral tomorrow. Good seeing you kids."

That's my dad. Man of few words.

My mom's not done with us yet, though. "It's different for women, and you know it. Men have time. They don't dry up as fast as us. They don't lose what makes them attractive to the opposite sex. Women have to strike young, while the iron's hot, as they say. Before all the good men are taken, and you lose your looks and ability to get a man."

This is just too much. I can't believe this bullshit. "Because a guy is only going to be interested in me for my looks? Is that really the kind of man you want me to end up with?"

"Women need security in this world, honey. It's how we survive in a man's world."

I stand, ready to be done with this. "Or, we could change the game. Make it a world for both men and women. How about that?"

I don't even wait for her response; instead I head for the car to unload my bag and settle into my old room for two nights. I wanted to get a hotel, but Mom insisted we stay here. "Why waste the money when your old rooms are all set up and ready?"

I conceded only because Tate insisted it would be okay. That we were adults now, on our own, and so things would be different.

But life doesn't change in the Michaels house. That's becoming painfully clear.

...

I'm sitting in my old room, posters of outdated bands lining the walls, my dresser mirror covered in pictures from my senior year in high school. Nothing has changed.

I feel like I'm in a shrine to myself.

I sit at my old oak vanity and pull a picture from the glass. It sticks for a moment before giving way under my fingers. It wasn't so terribly long ago that I was this girl dressed in pink taffeta, smiling big for the camera with my prom date at my side.

He seemed so important to me at the time. That night seemed so important to me. I remember we all snuck liquor into our punch and danced until they turned out the lights and kicked us out. It was a themed dance—as they all were back then—Under the Sea, and being held in the gym. It smelled like a combination of old gym socks and Elmer's glue. Everything sparkled.

We'd all chipped in and rented a hotel room for the after party, but somehow Lance and I got there first. I didn't lose my virginity that night—that would have been too cliché—but I'd come close. We ended up crossing that milestone a week later in the back of his old station wagon. I had bruises on my back the next day from the metal digging into me. It wasn't entirely pleasant, but it was done.

Sex has gotten a lot better since then. I have a theory that if your first time is in high school, or at least with a high schooler, it's bound to suck. Teenagers don't know what they're doing about much of anything, and sex is no exception.

I put the picture back in place, hiding the dust framed around it and explore the drawers and closets, marveling at what I considered cool to wear back then.

Tate walks in on me trying on the hideous taffeta gown from the picture.

"Nice look, sis. You heading to a blast-from-the-past party?" He closes the door and sits on the edge of my bed while I admire myself in the mirror.

"At least it still fits. The freshman fifteen didn't get me."

"And you look as glorious now as you did that night with, what was his name? Pants?"

I pick a stuffed animal from my corner dresser and throw it at him. "Lance. And I don't know why you were always such an ass to him."

"Because he was a tool. He probably still is. We could look him up while we're here, and you can see how he compares to Dr. Love. Who knows? Maybe you'll discover you've made a big mistake, and you really belong here, married to the new manager at Grease Monkey."

I try to imagine a universe in which that is my life, and the thought makes me shudder. "Turn around. I need to get out of this monstrosity."

He closes his eyes, and I peel the dress off and slip back into my own clothes before sitting on the bed next to him, both of us now leaning against the wall, our feet hanging off the side of the twin mattress covered in a lilac bedspread.

"So, how bad is it with Mom?"

He shrugs. "No worse than normal. Look, I know she's a pain in the ass, but give her a break, Kacie, she just lost her own mother. That can't be easy."

"Great, now I feel like an asshole for refusing to succumb to sexist bullshit." And I kind of do, except I'm not really sure what a proper response would have been. My mother and I are never going to agree on anything. Maybe I shouldn't have come.

I say as much to Tate, and he throws an arm over my shoulder. "I know she's glad you're here. Besides, we all need closure."

I lean my head against his shoulder and sigh. "You're right. You're a pain, but you're right."

"So, you planning on staying locked up in your room all night?" he asks, a mischievous look in his eyes.

"Well, it would be apropos of the old days, wouldn't it?"

"How about tonight we pretend to be adults and head out to those bars we could never get into when we were younger?"

I grin up at my brother, who suddenly seems so much smarter than I give him credit for. "Brilliant. And let's dress to the nines. Show Mansfield how people in Las Vegas like to party."

...

My mom nearly has a heart attack when we walk downstairs an hour later. I've got on a black leather mini-skirt and metallic silver tank top that doesn't cover much more than it has to. My hair is in a messy up-do, and my spiked heels scream "fuck me," though of course there will be no fucking of anyone tonight, expect in my dreams. Tate looks just as seductive in his bad-boy clubbing outfit.

"You're not going out in public like that, young lady," my mom says.

I laugh, until I realize she's dead serious.

"Mom, I'm an adult."

"Staying under my roof," she reminds me.

"At your insistence. It's not too late for us to get a hotel. And staying here as guests doesn't put us under your rules. Not anymore."

I'm not backing down on this one, and I think she finally realizes that, because she shrugs, sighs, and does all manner of non-verbals to indicate just how very not okay she is with all of this before stomping into the kitchen. "Don't drink and drive," she hollers.

"We won't," Tate says.

"I'm not walking in these heels," I tell him, but he just grins.

"Got it covered," he says.

When we walk outside, our taxi is waiting for us. We make it easy on ourselves and head downtown to hit up all the bars in one night. I can at least walk that far. And maybe drinking will help this time in hell pass more swiftly.

I don't know what I'm expecting when we arrive at the first hole-in-the-wall dive, but I realize I'm disappointed after we're there for a few minutes. Nothing looks or feels familiar. I don't recognize anyone from our past. I guess I wanted this to be an opportunity to, what? Show off to the poor people of Ohio? As soon as I think this, I realize what an asshole I am and feel ashamed.

When the bartender serves us another round of shots, I down mine quickly and eye the bathroom. "Be right back," I tell Tate, sliding off the barstool.

I'm washing my hands when someone comes in. No, it's not Sebastian. And no, I don't for a moment think (wish) it is. Okay? Just let it go. I'm not thinking of Sebastian Donovan.

Of course that's all a lie. I can't stop thinking of him, and I wish I'd taken him up on his offer to come with me. As much as I love Tate, when we're home like this, it all feels like some kind of time warp, and I feel eighteen again and under the thumb of my oppressive but well-intended parents. I need someone from outside all the insanity to give me some perspective, to ground me in the real world, not these memories of yesterday.

But I do a double-take at the blonde who saunters in, because I recognize her. When she sees me, she smiles wider. "Kacie? Kacie Michaels? Is that you?"

I dry my hands and walk over to her. "Leslie, hi. How are you?"

"I'm good, and look at you! So fancy. What are you doing here?"

I don't have a ton of memories of Leslie. She and I didn't hang in the same crowd, but we had enough classes together throughout high school that we were on a first name basis with each other.

"My grandmother died. Tate and I came for the funeral."

"Oh my God, Tate's here? Jill and the other girls are going to flip! I don't think any of us have stopped crushing on him since y'all left us for greener pastures."

I smile, ready for this conversation to be over. "He'll be delighted to hear it."

She links arms with me as I leave the bathroom. "You have got to tell us everything!"

"Didn't you need to use the bathroom?"

"Oh, I'm fine. Just came to freshen up. No biggie. This is way more important."

When Jill and the other "girls" see us coming out, they form a…what would a group of giggling girls who aren't really girls be? A gaggle? That sounds about right. They form a gaggle and surround me. I'm getting dizzy trying to keep track of who's talking to me, and I gesture for Tate to come rescue me. They're here to see him more than me, and as soon as they realize he's coming over, the gaggle moves as one beast towards my poor brother.

But he raises his arms and smiles big, and I know he'll survive the encounter with his typical Tate charm.

"Ladies, how lovely you all look tonight. What a great surprise seeing you here."

I can't help but smile at how well he can work a room. It's a skill, for sure. I take my drink before one of the gaggle girls grabs it and head outside for some fresh air. I text Tate, who's now surrounded and unapproachable, and let him know where I'm going.

You're lucky I love you so much.

Don't play that card, bro. I know you love the attention. And all the tits.

I can hear him laugh out loud at my text from inside, and I smile, sit down at an empty table and sip my drink, enjoying the chill in the air. It's nice being somewhere that doesn't feel like an inferno even at night. For once I'm not sweating through my clothing.

Over the next few hours, a couple of men try to chat me up, but I'm not interested in talking, and they leave me alone. When Tate finally emerges with a few new lipstick stains, I'm ready to go, and it looks like he is too.

The house is dark when we arrive home, and I feel like a teen again, sneaking in after curfew and skipping the third step on the stairs because it always squeaks.

That night I dream about proms and kisses under bleachers and shotgun weddings in Las Vegas.

...

My mother doesn't mention the night before, and neither do I. This is her day to mourn, and I vow to myself that I will be on my best behavior. I will bite my tongue even if it bleeds, to keep from mouthing off to her, no matter how asinine her comments are.

We are all quiet in the car over. I check my texts repeatedly, but Sebastian hasn't replied to my last few. I shouldn't be upset by this. I know he has work this weekend and can't text me 24/7, but I do hope I can talk to him today.

By the time we reach the graveside, the weight of the event begins to hit me.

It's not a large gathering, but there are enough people that I spend a good thirty minutes before the service saying hi to people who have known me since I was a child. I try not to look at the actual casket, but I'm eventually left no choice as the crowd moves me toward my seat, right in front of the casket and the oversized portrait of my grandmother.

When I see her picture there, her white hair perfectly coiffed, her lips smeared with that red lipstick that smelled funny, her blue eyes so sharp, I experience a surprising lump of emotion in my throat. She's in that coffin right now. Her body, lifeless and hollow, is just lying there. Dead.

My bottom lip quivers, and I look up, fighting tears, and stare straight into the eyes of Sebastian Donovan.

TWENTY FOUR
Perfect Match

I stand there, slack-jawed, until he comes over to me and pulls me into his arms. "Hello darling. I hope you don't mind that I'm here."

I wrap my arms around him and breathe in the deliciousness of his scent. "No. Not at all. But...how?"

He kisses me on my head, and I'm aware that everyone around me is staring, but I don't care one bit.

"I felt bad, you coming here alone, and I wanted to surprise you."

"I'm definitely surprised. And really glad you're here! Thank you."

I see my sister and mother staring at me, and I groan. "Prepare for the Michaels interrogation, though. And I hope meeting my family doesn't scare you away."

He chuckles under his breathe. "Darling, for you I'd fight dragons. A few family members are no problem."

"You haven't met my mother," I say as she comes over, clutching my sister's hand in hers. Tate is still talking to other family members and hasn't noticed the arrival of Sebastian.

Once my mom is close enough, she gives us a half-smile watered down by the grief still evident on her face. "Kacie, who is this handsome gentleman?"

"Mom, this is Sebastian. Sebastian, my mom, Martha, and sister, Jessica."

He shakes each of their hands. "Nice to meet you both."

My mom is clearly waiting for more information, but the priest arrives and is ready to start the service, so she returns to her seat, her focus back on the funeral.

Tate raises an eyebrow when he comes to sit next to me. "If I'd known you were bringing a date, I would have secured one for myself," he says.

"I didn't know. Now, hush, it's starting."

The service isn't long, but it does bring a tear or two to my eyes as friends of my grandmother speak about her charity work and how much she gave back to the community, especially in the last few years.

I realize that I didn't know the woman they're talking about. My memories of her are less than kind, but it seems she'd changed in her later years, and I feel a twinge of grief at the thought that now I'll never know the woman she chose to be toward the end of her life.

I steal a glance at my mother, who is dabbing her eyes with a handkerchief. I've always viewed my mother through the lens of my own childhood, but we're both adults now. I wonder whom I will see in her if I change that lens. Surely she's more than what my memories have made her.

...

Hitched

The post-funeral reception is at my parents' house, and I spend an hour introducing Sebastian to everyone as "my boyfriend," which just sounds lame, but what else can I say? The guy I married in Vegas? The guy I'm fucking? There aren't any really great ways to introduce someone you're in a relationship with once you become an adult, unless you're engaged or married. Someone should do something about this.

My mom lays it on thick, asking how long we've been together, if we're serious, if we plan on getting married, when we plan on having kids.

I want to die.

I want the ground to open up and swallow me.

But Sebastian handles her with ease and doesn't seem the least bit put off by all the expectations and questions.

As guests start to leave, Sebastian offers to help clean up the kitchen, but my mom shoos him away. "The ladies can handle it."

Tate hands Sebastian a beer, and they retire to the couch in the living room, casting sympathetic glances at me as my mother pulls me into the kitchen to clean and do dishes.

Women's work, obviously.

Thing is, I don't mind helping out. I just hate it being an expectation of my gender. "Shouldn't Jessica be here helping too?" I ask.

"Billy got a bloody nose, so she's taking care of the babies."

Of course, the one way to get out of helping in the kitchen is taking by care of the kids. Her husband is probably on the sofa drinking with the rest of the men.

But this kitchen duty doesn't go as I expect. As soon as we close the door, my mother turns to me with tears in her eyes and hugs me. "I'm so glad you're here, honey. I can't tell you how much I've missed you."

I hug her back, and we hold the embrace longer than normal. I relax, letting myself enjoy the feeling of my mother's arms around me, offering her whatever comfort I can through my own touch.

She sniffles, pulls away, and wipes a falling tear. "I'm sorry. I'm a bit emotional today."

I kick myself again for being such a bitch. "You have every right to be. I can't imagine what you're going through."

She waves her handkerchief at me. "Oh, you'd be glad to see me go. I know I'm just an old woman meddling in affairs that no longer concern me."

Ouch. "You're my mother. It's part of your job description." I try for a lighthearted tone, matched by a smile, and her lips crack into a small grin for just a moment.

"You know, when you were little, I knew you'd grow up to be something great."

I cast my eyes down. "I'm sorry I disappointed you."

She reaches for my hands. "Oh, honey, that's not what I meant. You haven't. I'm so proud of you. Working your way through school, starting a successful business, making your way in the world. I think you're amazing. I just…"

She wipes her eyes again, her mascara smudging. "I just don't want you to grow up and find yourself lonely. I know women these days don't need men to make them happy, and that's probably a good thing. And being married isn't always ice cream and roses, that's for sure. But there's comfort in knowing that you have someone by your side, come what may, who sees you and shares in the many memories you'll make together over the course of a lifetime. There's a certain beauty to that, and I want so badly for you to have that someday."

"Mom, I—"

"But I see now that I didn't need to worry. I can see clear as the nose on my face that you've already found it." She smiles so big her face stretches with the effort. "I don't know why you wanted to keep him a surprise, but you have sure made this day a happy one despite the sadness."

She pulls me into another hug as I try to swallow the lump in my throat.

"I know you two are going to be so very happy," she says in my ear. "And a doctor, no less. What a perfect match!"

TWENTY FIVE

The Devil Is in Me, and It's Coming Out

Tate and Sebastian bond during our trip home. I guess that's good. Maybe. I can't decide. I mean, if things last with Sebastian, then yes, I want my brother to like the man I end up with, obviously. But this leads to other questions of whether I'm ready for that or not, and I don't want to answer those just yet.

Still, it's a pleasant trip home, and I'm even happy to step into the arid Las Vegas heat. Mostly.

I think I did the right thing—not telling my mom about my doubts regarding my relationship. She seemed so happy, and it had been such a hard weekend for her. Sometimes it's better not to fight, to just walk away and let the other person think they've won.

Sebastian and I fall into our familiar routine once home. We finish each other's sentences, do cross word puzzles together in the morning paper, and cuddle on the couch at night, reading in silence.

I know Tate misses me, and I do pop home to spend time with him, and to work, but my nights are all Sebastian's.

Last night he cooked for me. I enjoyed every bite. I didn't feel the stomach cramps until this morning. Didn't know evil had taken root in my gut until it was too late to get to my own house, my own bed, my own bathroom, before it happened.

There are certain tests every relationship faces as it matures, but I am not ready for the one we're about to face.

This could be the end for us. I glare at myself in the mirror, hoping Sebastian doesn't wake up before I've figured out how to handle this disaster.

But before I can come up with a plan that would save us, a wave of nausea hits again, and I scramble to the toilet.

Unfortunately, I'm too late.

Vomit splatters everywhere. I can feel it in my hair, on my feet, the stink rising like something dead and rotting.

And I can't stop.

Then there's the knock on the door.

"You okay, darling?"

I would say yes, would tell him to go away, but as I open my mouth another wave of noxious sludge pours out of me.

The doorknob turns.

He walks in.

He's naked. We're both naked from the night before, but I'm the only one covered in last night's dinner.

Chicken marsala, if you were wondering. It's not nearly as good coming back up.

"Oh, honey, you look—"

I glare at him and dare him to finish the sentence.

He cocks his head. "Sick. You look sick. Since we ate the same thing yesterday, I'm guessing stomach flu. Let's clean you up and get you back to bed. Doctor's orders."

And my humiliation begins. I shower quickly, with his aid, and he dries me and wraps me up in blankets then brings me a bucket to puke into and seltzer water to help calm my stomach.

Then he cleans up the bathroom.

Now, I realize that he's a doctor and has likely seen worse. And that this is something everyone goes through at some point in his or her life. And that every relationship, if it lasts long enough, will be faced with the "in sickness" part of the vows—though I don't recall if we said that during our quickie wedding—but I'm not quite prepared to be an invalid in his presence. It's like the sexy has sloughed off my body revealing a scaly monster hiding underneath. And it smells like vomit.

Sebastian, however, doesn't bat an eye. For two days during the worst stomach flu of my life, he waits on me, caters to my every unspoken whim, and cleans up every trace of sick I leave behind.

And it makes my heart melt. Any man who can do that and still wants to be with you when it's all over is truly a keeper.

TWENTY SIX
Dead Poets

I didn't die.

That's the main thing, right? That I'm still alive and still with Sebastian. We survived the worst I could throw at us. Or throw up on us, as the case may be.

Now let's just put those last few days behind us and never speak of them again, okay? Great.

Moving on.

I'm browsing through Sebastian's reading selection while he pours us both coffee, but his choice in literature is…narrow. "Medical journals and historical military novels? Really? That's it?"

He chuckles. "It's enough. And I do have one Sherlock Holmes book somewhere around here."

I raise an eyebrow and accept the coffee. "One?"

"It's a collection, so it counts as more."

"You need to expand your literary tastes," I tell him as I scan one of his medical books.

"I think my literary tastes are fine as they are."

I put the book back and turn to him. "This could compromise the integrity of our relationship if this isn't handled quickly. An intervention is in order."

He kisses my forehead fondly. "What did you have in mind?"

"Let's go to a bookstore," I suggest.

"A bookstore?"

"Yeah, you know, one of those big buildings where they keep all the books, but you have to pay if you want to leave with them. I know they're a bit archaic in our dot-com world, but surely Vegas still has one or two if we look hard enough."

He grins. "I'm sure there are. That sounds like fun."

I pull out my phone and Google bookstores. Because I was serious about the dot-com world. I love reading but can't remember the last time I went to an actual brick and mortar bookstore.

"We have a few promising choices," I tell him. "There's a Barnes & Noble on West Charleston...that would be a predictable choice."

"Entirely too predictable," he says.

"Oh, these look more exciting. How about Amber Unicorn Books on Decatur, or Dead Poet Bookstore on Rainbow Boulevard? I wonder if we'll spot any actual unicorns?"

"Or dead poets," he says.

"Or those. So, what's your vote? Dead poets or the rare unicorn?"

I follow him to the kitchen and sit on a stool as he rinses our now-empty coffee cups out. "I'm going to have to cast my vote with the Dead Poets."

I jump up off the stool, then immediately regret it as my stomach is still a bit wibbly-wobbly from the days that shall not be spoken of. "I knew you'd pick that one. *Dead Poet's Society* is your favorite movie."

"Indeed!"

We leave the house in under ten minutes and arrive at a charming used and rare bookstore that is larger than I expected. While a bit dusty, it has the feel of a place that has hosted many deep conversations and insightful meanderings through classic literature.

I love it instantly.

Dotted through the store are nooks for reading, clusters of chairs and couches for group meetings, and even a chess board for those who want to kill some time honing their strategy skills.

I run my hands over the old leather-bound books and sigh, breathing in the smell of paper and ink. "I should come to bookstores more often. I forgot how much I enjoy them."

Sebastian takes out his phone and snaps a picture of me, then smiles. "You look radiant among the classics, Ms. Michaels."

After browsing the titles for over an hour and purchasing a few to take home, I challenge Sebastian to a game of chess.

"Right now?" He raises an eyebrow.

"Obviously." I sit in one chair, and he sits down across from me, dropping our bag of books next to him.

"I have to warn you, I'm quite good," he says.

"And I should warn you, I'm not bad myself."

"Very well then," he gestures gallantly, "ladies first."

The game is a quiet one, each of us fiercely concentrating as we attempt to out maneuver each other.

When he takes my pawn, I pump my fist and wipe out his rook. But then he sneaks in and puts my queen in jeopardy, so I rethink my next move and am forced to go on the defensive.

We circle each other like alley cats. Each of us pushing the other into offensive or defensive, depending on the move.

His mind is keen, and he doesn't miss much as he watches me study the board. We are both down to a skeleton crew defending our kings. The game will be over in a few more moves.

I think I have him, that I've surely won, but at the last moment he sacrifices everything and manages to not only save his king but puts me in checkmate at the same time.

I look up at him and smile, because that move shows me something about him, something real and deep. It shows me that when he commits to something, he goes all in. He risks it all to win what he wants.

And somehow, for some reason, this man wants me.

TWENTY SEVEN
Meet the Parents

Tate laughs at me, and I throw a dirty shirt at his face. "If you're not going to help, then go away."

We're in my bedroom, where I've packed and repacked for my weekend trip with Sebastian about ten times. The weeks have flown by, and now it's time to go meet his family and witness his uncle getting married. When Vi committed me to this, I didn't know how much would happen in the intervening weeks. My grandmother dying. Sebastian coming to Ohio. The forty-eight hours of ick that shall not be discussed.

Everything about our relationship feels so different now, so much more intimate, but still, I'm nervous as hell.

Tate tosses the shirt into the laundry hamper by my closet. "You're only going for a few days. You don't have to pack everything you own."

I assess my suitcase and realize he's right. I've packed almost everything. This is ridiculous. I'm a pro at packing. I can go weeks with just a backpack and some gum. In fact, I did just that in Europe the summer after graduating college. Best summer ever.

But now? I can't figure out which dress to pack for the actual wedding, let alone the dinner rehearsal, or what to wear when I actually arrive there and meet his family for the first time. We've talked a bit about his life growing up. I know he's close to his little sister, and his younger brother is more the black sheep of the family. I know he loves his parents. But I don't know what they're going to think of me. And it scares the shit out of me.

I hold up a blue dress and an off-white skirt suit. "Which one?"

"Depends, do you want to look like someone from the cast of Smurfs or an unmarried crazy cat lady?"

I look down at the choices and then scowl at him. "You have no taste."

He hops off the bed and crosses the room to my closet. In a few moments, he pulls out a tasteful lavender sleeveless dress with lace and pearls. "This one."

I fold it into my bag and find the shoes that match. After tossing all the extra clothes I won't need—including a heavy coat and boots, because where do I think I'm going? Sebastian said his parents live only an hour away. My bag is much lighter and more appropriate for a weekend away.

Just in time, too. The doorbell rings, and I know it's him.

"Will you get that and tell him I'll be right down?"

Tate leaves, and I quickly change into a pale yellow sundress with sandals and twist my hair into a braid.

Sebastian looks casually delicious at the bottom of the staircase as I come down, bag in hand.

"Hello there, darling. You look ravishing."

His voice melts me.

We kiss, and he takes my bag. "Ready to go?"

I nod, waving at Tate who's already flopped on the couch watching something on television. "Call me if you have any problems with the party this weekend," I tell him as I open the front door.

He looks up and smiles. "We got it covered. You go have fun."

...

It takes about an hour to get to his family's house, and during that time I grill Sebastian about everyone I'm going to meet. I don't want to make any social faux pas the first time I meet them.

He laughs at my nervousness and pats my hand. "You're going to be fine. They'll love you as much as I do."

I gulp. There's that word again. Love. We haven't actually said the words "I love you"—at least not since the night I can't remember—but he has casually tossed it out there, and it makes my heart beat too fast each time.

Do I love him? Is it possible to fall in love this fast? I know I care for him. I know I'm going to miss him dreadfully if this ends. But love? That's such a big word. Such a big commitment. It terrifies me. I've always seen love as something that takes from you the core of who you are. When you love someone, they have power over you. They can hurt you. They can control you, even if subtly. Everything changes, and I don't want that to happen to me.

I look over at Sebastian as he drives. His profile is strong, chiseled, his skin tanned, his eyes so very beautiful. Everything about this man is too good to be true. I'm waiting for the other shoe to drop. As it always inevitably does.

...

His family home takes my breath away.

Literally.

"*This* is where you grew up?" I ask as we pull onto the property.

"Yes. Home sweet home."

"Mansion sweet mansion, more like." I think about the small farmhouse I grew up in. It would fit in one of the bathrooms in this place, by the looks of it. "How big is it?"

As we drive down a long road to the front of the house, we pass a rectangular fountain spraying dancing water into the sky, lit up by multi-colored lights. The house itself curves around to either side, with large, oval floor-to-ceiling windows everywhere.

"The property is 40 acres, and the main house is almost twelve thousand square feet."

I'm not even sure how to visualize that many feet in my head, square or not. "Main house? There's more than one house?"

He nods as we get out of the car and grab our bags. "Yes, there are two guest houses in the back. My brother lives in one, but my sister chose to stay in the main house."

The moment we walk in I can see why his sister would want to stay here. The ornate double doors open wide to a cream entryway framed by cream and wrought iron stairways on either side.

Above us a chandelier casts lights off the walls and showers us with fragments of that light reflecting off of crystals.

The first person I meet is his little sister, Clara, who comes running in and throws herself into her big brother's arms. "Sebastian! It's so good to see you."

He drops his suitcase and wraps his arms around her, swinging her around like a child. "You too, kiddo. Sorry it's been so long."

She steps out of his embrace to look at him, and I take the moment to study her. She's beautiful. More petite than her brother with fine bones and pale skin contrasted against dark shoulder-length hair and large hazel eyes. She wears glasses perched on her nose as if she's been reading and forgot to take them off.

When she turns to look at me, I tense, worried this lovely elf of a girl will find me wanting in some way, not good enough for her amazing brother.

Instead, she smiles warmly and moves in to hug me.

I'm used to PDA with Tate and Vi, so this doesn't bother me at all, and I return her hug enthusiastically.

"It's so good to meet you," Clara says. "Sebastian couldn't stop talking about you last time he called to let us know he'd be bringing you."

I eye Sebastian, unaware that he'd been talking me up to his family. I guess it makes sense though. He couldn't just bring me unannounced to a wedding. "It's nice meeting you too," I tell her honestly. "Sebastian sings your praises as well."

She beams and grabs my hand. "Let me show you around while my brother takes your luggage upstairs."

Sebastian scowls. "Stealing her away already?"

"We need girl time to get to know each other. Mom and Dad aren't home yet from their errands, but it shouldn't be too much longer."

"And Matt?"

She frowns for the first time. "You know Matt. We'll be lucky if he deigns to honor us with his presence at all this weekend." She makes shooing motions at him. "Now go!"

Sebastian looks to me as if to ask if I'm okay. I nod and smile, confident that Clara and I will get along just fine. He leans in, takes my face in both of his hands, and kisses me. "I'll miss you," he says in a husky voice that makes me weak in the knees.

Clara giggles as Sebastian takes the stairs two at a time, suitcases in both hands.

I hate to be away from him as well, but I link arms with Clara and wonder if this will be my chance to get the inside scoop on the sexy doctor who is coming close to stealing my heart.

...

The house is tastefully decorated in shades of off-white with black accents everywhere. I love it. But when we go outside and explore the stables, I nearly die.

Horses. I loved horses when I was a child—what little girl doesn't?—but I rarely got to ride one, despite growing up in the farm land of Mansfield, Ohio.

Clara hands me a carrot to give to a beautiful white filly, who eats it greedily from my palm.

"Does Sebastian like riding?" I ask, trying to imagine him on one of these horses.

She grins. "Loves it. Hard to imagine, right? Mr. Big Shot Doctor astride a horse, but he's been riding since he was old enough to walk. You should have him take you for a ride while you're here."

I pat the horse's nose as we move on with our tour. "Maybe I will."

As we walk through manicured gardens with a variety of plants, trees and flowers, Clara turns to me. "Sebastian said you two got married."

Damn him. He should have warned me they knew. "Yes, in a manner of speaking. But it will be annulled soon. I've already sent in the paperwork."

"I've never seen him like this with anyone else," she says softly.

"Like what?" My heart is aching.

"Happy," she says simply.

We sit on a bench and watch the light around us change as the sun begins to set.

"Try not to break his heart," she begs, her eyes wide and earnest. "He's already had that happen once."

"Was he happy with her. Before?"

Clara pauses, thinking, before she shrugs. "He had moments where things were okay, but they never seemed a fit, you know? The pregnancy gave them the illusion of closeness. Gave them a reason to make it official, I guess. But, she...she's so calculating and cold. I could never imagine them together forever. And then the baby died, and she showed her true colors."

"I know what you mean. The few times I've met her she's been…a bitch."

Clara laughs. "I was trying to be delicate, but yes, you've nailed it on the head. She's a world-class bitch. I'm glad she'll never be my sister-in-law."

She gives me a look that says she hopes I *will* be, and I don't know what I'm feeling.

Instead I change the subject. "This house, these grounds, they are impressive. Sebastian never mentioned what your father did for a living."

"He teaches sixth grade English at the local high school," she says.

I stare at her. "Seriously?"

She nods.

"But…" I don't know how to ask my next question without sounding shallow.

"How do we afford all this?"

I give a nod. Exactly. How?

"I'm surprised Sebastian didn't tell you. This isn't from my dad. Our mom is a dot-com billionaire."

Suddenly everything is cast in a different light. And I realize how incredibly sexist my assumption was. "Your mom? I'm sorry, I must sound like a complete ass."

"Don't worry; it's a common misconception."

"Did she do all this before having kids?" There are so many more questions buried in that one seemingly innocuous question.

"Nope. They started out lower middle class, and she did programming while we were little. I'd just been born when her big success happened."

"That's…incredible. She truly managed to have it all."

Clara nods. "That's what I love most about her. That she didn't sacrifice her dreams and goals to have us, and she didn't sacrifice us to accomplish her dreams."

...

When we arrive back at the main house, Mr. and Mrs. Donovan are sitting in the living room having a drink with Sebastian. He stands when he sees us come in, and once again takes a moment to brush my lips with his. Clara is nearly beside herself with glee at our public display.

He takes my hand and turns to his parents. "Mom, Dad, this is Kacie Michaels. Kacie, this is Sylvia and Robert Donovan. The people who made me." He grins like a fool, and I love him for it.

I let go of his hand to shake theirs. "It's nice to meet you both. Thank you for having me this weekend. Your house is absolutely lovely."

Sylvia wears a classy beige suit. Robert is dressed more casually in khakis and a polo shirt. They are a handsome couple, both dark haired and clear skinned. Sebastian gets his blue eyes from his mother. Robert shares Clara's hazel.

"We're so glad you could come, Kacie," says Sylvia.

Robert offers me a glass of wine, and I accept and sit next to Sebastian across from his parents.

"Sebastian was just telling us about the business you own, planning bachelor parties," Robert says.

I'm never embarrassed by what I do, but sitting there with this family, all of whom have accomplished so much, I wonder if they'll think I'm good enough for their son. "My twin and I co-own it," I clarify.

Robert nods. "What made you decide on that path?"

"We always knew we wanted to have our own company and work for ourselves. It's why we went to business school after graduation. We didn't expect this exact business, but when one of our friends in college got married, he asked us to plan his party, and we got creative. We discovered not only a talent for it, but also a passion for it as well. That's when our idea for Hitched started to solidify."

Sylvia smiles. "That's wonderful. I applaud anyone who pursues their passion and follows their heart."

"I agree," Robert says. "An entrepreneurial spirit is important for success in this world, but only if you love what you do."

Their attitude is so refreshing I almost cry tears of relief. I expected judgment, criticism, or at least silent condemnation, and instead I've been received with smiles and open arms. I can see why Sebastian loves his family so much.

I'm starting to love them too.

...

The wedding isn't until Sunday with the rehearsal dinner on Saturday night. So when we wake the next morning, I'm excited to spend the day with Sebastian and his family before everyone arrives tonight for the festivities.

Robert is making breakfast for everyone when we go downstairs. I'm dressed casually, per Sebastian's request. Jeans and a t-shirt it is until it's time to dress up for the dinner tonight.

I'm surprised to see his dad cooking, though. "You don't have someone who handles the cooking?" I ask Sebastian before we reach earshot of his dad.

"We do, but my dad likes cooking, so he usually does the breakfasts and weekend meals."

I'm more and more impressed with his family.

We sit at the bar in the spacious kitchen as Robert hands us each a plate and serves up omelets. "I hope you like eggs," he says.

"I do!" With the first bite I know where Sebastian learned to cook.

Robert joins us, and I ask about Clara and Sylvia.

"They're out shopping for tonight," he says. "Though I can't imagine what else we need. Sylvia has been planning every detail of her brother's wedding for months. I'm pretty sure she's paying the wedding planner just to run errands."

I laugh, then realization dawns. "Is there going to be a bachelor party tonight?"

Sebastian shakes his head. "They did that last week. They didn't want this weekend to be so busy."

"A lot of couples are choosing to have their parties early for that very reason," I inform him. Noticing that everyone is done with their food, I get up and collect the plates.

Robert tries to stop me, but I insist. "You cooked. You shouldn't have to clean as well." Growing up my mom did all the cooking and the cleaning. It never seemed fair.

Sebastian dries as I wash, and Robert turns on music, a light jazz, and sits down with a book. "What are you two kids up to today?" he asks.

I look to Sebastian, since I don't know what he has planned yet.

He smiles mischievously. "Horseback riding. I want to show her the lake."

"That sounds fun."

"We're going horseback riding?"

He nods and leans in to whisper in my ear. "While I'd prefer you ride me, I think this could also be fun."

I blush and remember last night. We made love with his parents in the house, which felt naughty and forbidden, and I tried to be very quiet despite Sebastian's assurance that no one would hear us in this huge house.

As if he can tell what I'm thinking, he brushes his lips against my neck, his tongue flicking ever so gently against my skin as the warmth of his breath tickles me.

I melt against his broad chest as his arms encompass me.

"Ready to have some fun?" he asks.

"Depends on what you have in mind?" I'm imagining us naked, sheets tangled around us as our bodies rub against each other.

But he guides me outside to the horses, and I see he's got an entirely different fantasy at play here. Which is fine. This probably isn't the time for sexy. Unfortunately. Because this man, this fucking man, makes me want him all the fucking time, and it's driving me nuts.

He stops by the horse I fed yesterday. Winnie. She's beautiful, and it seems as if she remembers me as she pushes her head against my hand. "Sorry girl, I didn't bring treats this time."

Her soft lips explore my empty hands before she settles for me petting her as Sebastian saddles her for a ride.

"Who's riding her?" I ask.

"We both are," he says as he finishes up.

"Really?" I raise an eyebrow at him. This isn't what I'd been expecting.

"Really. Hop on, my dear."

I'm not as graceful as I would like, but I manage to mount her without too much embarrassment. Sebastian eases himself up as if he's spent his life doing this. Which, I guess he has. His chest is pressed against my back, cock stiffening against my ass. I snuggle in against him as he takes the reins and clicks his tongue at Winnie.

The day is hot, which isn't surprising, but the breeze from riding cools me, and I enjoy the feel of the wind in my hair as we gallop over acres of his family's property.

When Sebastian slows the horse, I think we're stopping, but instead he frees one of his hands and wraps his arm around my waist, his mouth at my ear. "I want to make love to you under my favorite tree by the lake," he says as his hand slips into my jeans and below my panties.

Our thighs are pressed together, our bodies connected as his finger finds my clit and rubs it. When he moves his hand lower, sliding one, then two fingers into my pussy as he continues his attention on my clit with this thumb, I moan, leaning back into him. "You're bad," I tell him breathlessly.

"You make me want to do bad things, Ms. Michaels," he says.

The movement of the horse under us pushes his fingers deeper. His teeth bite into my neck, not roughly, but enough that the shock of it combined with his fingers forces my body into a coil of nerves and tightly contracted muscles looking for release.

When I come, it is fast and hard. The horse picks up pace, either at Sebastian's instruction or on her own, I'm not sure. I'm lost in a wave of pleasure as his fingers bring me to a greater and greater climax.

He timed this well. We arrive at a lake, with a large weeping willow tree shading a grassy knoll. I'm still shaking with the aftershocks of my orgasm when he stops and slides off the horse, helping me down. He leads Winnie to the water for a drink, then ties her near some nice looking grass.

I sink into the grass under the shade, my body a noodle after his naughtiness.

But he gives me no time to recover as he moves between my legs and pulls off my shirt. "I missed your tits," he says, freeing them from my bra and tossing it to the side.

"They missed you." I unbuckle his pants and pull them open, freeing his hard, throbbing cock.

Shafts of sunlight sneak through the leaves, warming my breasts as he lays me down and frees me from my jeans and underwear.

Soon we are both naked, the soft grass under us, shaded from the worst of the sun as water laps near our feet and birds sing, the only sounds are of nature and our breathing as he places his cock at the entrance of my pussy.

I love how he feels when he first enters me. That sensation of being stretched and filled, of his hard cock pushing into me until we are one.

And then he pulls me up and onto his lap, both of us sitting up, our chests pressed together, faces inches apart as I ride him, his hips moving in rhythm to mine, and he is so deep I can feel him everywhere. His hands explore my back and hips, tug on my hair, cover my body.

Hitched

My nails dig into his shoulders. I know he'll have marks later, but I don't care. I can't stop. Everything is building again. It's almost too much. I don't know how my body can contain these feelings, both physical and emotional, as he locks eyes with me, his cobalt blue gaze piercing me as we come together in the shade of his childhood tree.

...

That night I gladly join in, helping to set up tables, decorate and get things ready for the rehearsal dinner on the grand pack porch. It feels good to be doing something familiar. Setting up for parties is my job, after all.

We finish in plenty of time and are enjoying a glass of wine as the sun sets, and guests begin to show up.

And I finally get to meet the elusive Matt.

He arrives just before his uncle and future aunt, wearing torn jeans, a black leather jacket and carrying a motorcycle helmet. He's just as handsome as his brother, with the same blue penetrating eyes, but he carries himself differently, more like he's ready to get into a bar fight at the first opportunity.

When Sebastian introduces us, Matt's eyes wander up and down my body before landing on my eyes. "Nice to meet you," he says, smirking.

I squeeze his hand too hard and smile. "I'd say the same, but I prefer meeting people who don't blatantly disrespect me by deliberately ogling my body before making eye contact."

Clara chokes on the sip of wine she's taking, and Sebastian can't hold in a laugh as his brother drops my hand

and frowns for a moment before smiling again. "You're right. That was rude of me. I apologize. It's good to see my brother has found a woman his equal."

I'm surprised by his change of tone, as is everyone else by the looks of it, but Matt ignores us all and pours himself a glass of something decidedly stronger than wine.

"When's the party starting?" he asks.

Sylvia checks her watch. "Within the next ten minutes. You're just in time. I'm glad you could make it."

I'm surprised she doesn't lay on more guilt than that, but then, she doesn't seem the type to use emotional manipulation to get her way. Whatever Matt's issues are, his family seems to have learned to accept him as he is. Warts and all.

...

The dinner is a blur. I meet too many people to remember everyone's names, and though Sebastian's uncle and his fiancée greet me, they are monopolized by nearly everyone there, so I hang back, not wanting to intrude on their time with family and friends. I don't mind though; it's nice to see Sebastian relaxed around his family. I like watching him laugh at someone's joke or tell a story about something that happened long ago.

The night is magical for me in some unnamable way. There's something about being around this kind of family, the kind of family that loves unconditionally and can laugh together and enjoy spending time with each other. I wish Tate were here to be a part of this, to know that this is even possible.

It's not that our family life was awful. We weren't abused. Our parents loved us and still do. I think the challenge for us both was growing up knowing we didn't fit in at all with the rural Ohio life and the values our family cherished. We never established roots because we both knew from the earliest age that we wouldn't stay. And we didn't. The moment we graduated high school we were out of there, and we haven't gone back for more than the briefest visits.

Our parents didn't pay for our education or any of our expenses. We took out loans, worked our asses off, and lived on ramen noodles and power bars for entire semesters, just to make it to our dreams.

And that's fine. I'm a stronger person because of that journey. But I've never felt as at ease with my own family as I do right now with Sebastian's, and that makes me feel equal parts joy and sadness.

As the dinner winds down, and everyone has memorized where they're supposed to be tomorrow, Sebastian comes over to me, slipping an arm around my shoulder. "Everything okay? You seem quiet."

I rest my head against his chest. "I'm great, actually. Just enjoying this beautiful night. You're lucky you know, to grow up here."

"It's a nice house," he says.

I shake my head. "That's not what I mean. Here, with these people, in this love and joy. Not everyone gets that."

He lifts my chin with his finger and looks into my eyes. "You will always have that with me, Kacie."

...

Over three hundred people have RSVP'd for the wedding. There are tents and chairs everywhere, and the backyard has been transformed into a fairytale landscape by the time I make it downstairs. "I can't believe how much is already done," I say to Clara, who is on breakfast duty this morning. Which, for her, involves pouring coffee and a bowl of cereal.

Works for me.

By late morning Sebastian and I are both dressed and ready to go, as is everyone else in the Donovan family. As guests begin to arrive, I slip into the kitchen to help with moving food and setting up, even though they've hired a catering company to handle everything. I still want to feel useful. I'm not used to being at a party and not working.

The service starts promptly and is short, simple and beautiful. The bride is stunning, and the groom looks so happy his face is about to crack from that smile. I love it.

When they say, "I do," Sebastian and I glance at each other. And for a fraction of a moment, I have another memory from that night we met. I remember looking into his eyes as we said, "I do." Just a glimpse of the memory, but the emotions it brings back is enough to take my breath away.

I knew I loved him that night.

That's why I married him.

And I still love him now.

TWENTY EIGHT

Heart to Heart

That night, after all the guests have left, I find myself sitting outside at an empty table, plates of half-eaten wedding cake my only company. It's a balmy night, and the white lights that have created such a magical setting for a wedding continue to twinkle in the dark. Sebastian accompanied his dad to take home a few intoxicated guests, so I'm left with my thoughts, which isn't a bad thing.

Surrounded by people all day, mostly strangers, it feels good to grab a few minutes of solitude.

"Kacie, there you are." Sylvia walks out of the house holding two cups of coffee and smiles at me. "We wondered where you'd disappeared to."

"Just enjoying the night," I say.

"Would you prefer to be left alone? Or might I join you?"

I gesture to the seat next to me. "I'd love the company." It's true. I've wanted to spend more time with Sebastian's mother, but it's been such a busy weekend.

She hands me a cup of coffee. "Figured we could all use one after so much champagne and wine."

My head is still a bit buzzed from drinking, and I accept the coffee gratefully. The first sip burns down my throat in that oh-so-delicious way that only coffee can. I sigh with contentment. "This is excellent coffee," I say.

"Thank you. I worked as a barista in college. Guess my time there paid off."

The shock of imagining her working in a coffee shop must have shown in my eyes because she laughed. "We haven't always lived like this. This much opulence…it's a gift, but we started out modest, struggling, like most people."

"Clara said you're the one who made enough for…all this? Through your programming?"

She nods. "Yes. It was a combination of hard work, talent and luck. I had an idea, made it happen and became one of the few female dot-com billionaires of my time."

"I can't imagine growing up like this." To imagine this house as my childhood house seems impossible.

"I can't either, to be honest," she says. "We've tried to instill an ethic of hard work in our kids, to make sure they know not to take this kind of wealth for granted. Clara and Sebastian took to it. Matt…well, he has other challenges, but he's a good kid."

"What was Sebastian like as a kid?" I ask, dying to know more about this man I'm falling in love with.

She offers a sweet smile full of motherly love. "He was always such a nurturer. We weren't surprised when he chose medicine as his vocation, and I was glad, then, that we had the money to get him the best education. I didn't want my kids weighed down by college debt."

"He said it was partly because of Clara's heart condition?"

She takes a sip of her coffee and nods. "Yes, but I think he would have chosen medicine regardless. He definitely picked pediatric heart surgery because of his sister. They were all very young when we found out Clara needed a new heart. She was just a baby, and Matt and Sebastian doted on her as if they'd made her themselves. Those boys fought about everything, even when they were little, but when it came to Clara, they found common ground. They'd do anything to protect her."

Her words sound thick, and her eyes gloss over as she discusses the past. "It was a close call. We almost lost her. It was then that Sebastian came to us with his plan. With a little face so serious, he told us he'd decided to donate his heart to Clara so she could live." Her voice chokes at this, and I can feel tears burn the back of my eyes as well.

"He said he knew he couldn't live without a heart, but he was okay with that. He'd had a longer life, he argued. And he wanted his sister to have that too."

I lay my hand on hers, and she squeezes it and half-smiles at me. "Of course our hearts broke at this, and we had to tell him that's not how it worked, that people who are still alive and healthy can't donate organs they need to survive. You should have seen his face when he realized he couldn't save Clara. I cried myself to sleep that night, for all of our children. But the next day, we received our miracle. They found a donor for Clara."

Someone else had to die to give up that heart. I'm sure that's a thought that weighs on Clara and her family. What a blessing that person and their family gave to save the life of a stranger.

"When Clara came home the first night with her new heart, Sebastian insisted we get him a stethoscope so he could listen to it. Again, with his very serious little boy face, he put it on and held it up to her heart. After a few moments, he took it off and smiled. 'Her heart is strong,' he said. 'She's going to be okay.'"

"Sebastian never told me any of this," I say, picturing it all so clearly in my mind.

"I'm not surprised. He's very private with some things in his life. That was a challenging time for all of us, something we don't often revisit."

"How did you manage it all?" I ask. "Three kids, one of whom was so sick, a husband, and such an intense career."

"The way you handle anything," she says. "Every day I made choices about how to prioritize my time. There were times, when Clara was the most sick, that my work took second place to being with my children. But there were also times when work drove me. I didn't always do it well, the work or the family stuff, but I did the best I could with what I had. My husband has always been very supportive, both as a husband and a father, and he knew when he married me that my career mattered a lot, and I would need time and attention to build it."

"Did he mind? That you had this career that ended up making more than he does?"

She laughs. "Not in the least. He's never been one to care much about money. He was just glad we didn't go broke from the medical bills. He's always appreciated the privileges my career has given us, even if it's not something he would have sought for himself."

"Do you think Sebastian is like his father in that way?"

She smiles knowingly and pats my hand. "If you're worried that Sebastian will put his career before yours, don't. I know my son, and he would want the woman he marries to have her own life, her own dreams and hopes and aspirations. And I also know that he's hoping that woman is you."

TWENTY NINE
Leap of Faith

You have a date tomorrow night

I reply to Sebastian's text, knowing I should be working, but unable to resist a short break. It's been two days since we returned from his parent's house, and two days since I've seen him.

Really? Who's the lucky guy?

His text comes almost instantly.

My cock.

I laugh, and Tate gives me the evil eye. "I'm no cock block," he says, "but shit needs to get done. Or did you forget we're jumping out of an airplane tomorrow?"

Yeah, right. Forgetting would be a blessing. Joey's latest party is our craziest yet, and I've been going over safety rules all day. The last thing our business needs is someone turning into a pancake because they can't open their parachute. "I'll finish up and confirm the reservations." I give him my own evil eye. "Cock block."

He gives me the finger and gets back to work at his desk.

I text Sebastian.

I'm sorry, but your cock will have to reschedule. I have a party tomorrow night.

Can we come?

I type away, as Tate sighs at me.

Who the heck is we?

My cock and I.

I giggle, then bite my lip as thoughts of Sebastian inside me fill my mind.

No, sorry. But I'll see you next week. And then, I promise you will *come.*

We're looking forward to it.

After a brief pause, I get another text.

My parents really liked you.

I smile.

I really liked them too. Now stop texting me. You're distracting me from working, and you're turning my brother into a cock block, which is something he swore he'd never become.

Okay. I'll stop, but my cock wants me to remind you we have a date next week.

I'll put it on my schedule.

I try to get back to work, searching for the phone number of the restaurant we booked, but my thoughts keep going to Sebastian and his family. His mother balanced a time consuming career *and* a family. Am I ready for that?

Despite the memory of Sebastian and I horseback riding—and his fingers—I manage to get my work done and spend the evening watching skydiving videos on YouTube. I'm still stressed when I fall asleep.

The party at the hotel room, the restaurant, goes off without a hitch. But as Joey and the groom get ready to jump out of an airplane, I'm biting my nails.

"Don't worry," says Tate, his arm around me because I insisted we stay close. "If you die, I promise I'll keep the business running."

I elbow him in the stomach. "Asshole. I'm writing you out of my will."

The groom jumps out, followed by Joey, and I cover my eyes with my hands.

"Oh shit," says Tate softly. "They didn't make it."

"Fuck you, motherfucker," I say, because of course they made it. Right?

"Okay, you're next," says our instructor as he waves me to the door. I move fast, because it's the only way I'll be able to get through this. I could have chosen to stay on the ground, but I believe you should try most things at least once. Ever since I started Hitched, I've tried many things I never thought I would. And as I stand on the edge, I realize there's something else I'm ready to try.

I'm ready to try balancing Hitched and Sebastian.

And I jump.

THIRTY

Bitch Charming

"I'm officially divorced," I say, holding the annulment papers that arrived this morning.

Tate walks out of the kitchen, morning coffee in hand, smirking. "And I thought you two were so happy together."

I slide the papers into a black box I purchased a few days ago. "We're happy, but not ready for marriage. At least, I'm not."

"So are you breaking it off?"

I shake my head, drop my wedding ring into the box and cover it with a handwritten note.

I hope to wear this again, when I'm ready. But for now, I have a date with Dr. Sexy.

Tate snickers over my shoulder. Bastard must have read the note.

I shut the box and turn on him, frowning. "What?"

"You're going to end up with this guy. You're practically dying to have his babies."

"No. I'm not." *At least not yet. I always liked the name Jason for a boy...* I stop thinking about what may never happen and wrap the box with a white ribbon.

"You're a bad liar," says Tate. "Just promise me one thing."

"I might. What is it?"

"Invite me to the wedding this time, okay?"

We both laugh as I grab my shoes and purse, the black box wrapped under my arm. As Tate turns on the morning news, I walk out the door and drive to Sebastian's house. I have a note to deliver.

...

As I pull up in driveway, my cellphone rings. "Yes?"

"Hello, I need to schedule a bachelor party." His voice is excited, and I don't recognize it.

It's a new client. I would squeal if he couldn't hear me. "Sure, what day do you have in mind?"

"This Wednesday. I know it's a little last minute, but we just couldn't wait to get married, you know?"

"All too well," I say, still shocked I married a one-night stand. But of course, that one-night stand was Sebastian, so normal rules don't apply, right?

"Great, so can you schedule it?"

I glance over my mental calendar. Shit. Sebastian and I planned to go to *Le Reve* on Wednesday. He's already bought the tickets, and they aren't cheap. But I can't ask this guy to reschedule his wedding. We'll just have to go later, and I'll buy new tickets from the money I get from this job. "No problem," I say. "I'll call you back tomorrow to discuss the details."

"Thank you."

Excited about my new client and holding the black box behind my back, I head for Sebastian's door. I ring the bell, once, twice, three times, but he doesn't answer. Is he not home?

I could text him, but I don't want to spoil my surprise visit, so I check around the house, hoping he's in the back. I hear splashing. Bingo. I look over the fence, and see Sebastian stepping out of the pool, water dripping down his muscled back. Here's the man I'm considering spending the rest of my life with.

And he's walking straight toward Celene.

THIRTY ONE
Fall Out

What is the fucking bitch doing at his house? I'm about to call out, when Sebastian reaches for Celene. HUGS. HER. What the fuck?

Celene has tears streaming down her face. Great. She's so happy she's fucking crying. What the fuck is going on?

I want to confront both of them, yell at them, but no words come to my mouth. My throat feels swollen, and my mouth too dry.

Maybe they're getting back together. Maybe I'm just misunderstanding things.

I'm ready to punch her. To punch them.

But then I look closer. I see how they fit together. How they share something he and I will never share. I remember her words that day in the hospital. Will I ever be the person Sebastian really needs? Will I ever truly be a part of the most important thing in his life? His medicine.

I thought I could. But looking at them now...I am kidding myself. We were playing house in a make-believe world. None of it was real.

What I'm looking at now, that's real. They've got history. They made a fucking child together. They have everything he and I will never have.

Celene is perfect for Sebastian. Or at least, she's better than me. She's a doctor, and she's ready for marriage. I'm struggling to build a business and may not be ready to marry for years. Fuck her. Fuck both of them.

Before they can notice me, I storm back to my car, crumpling the black box in my hands. My eyes swell with tears as I step on my foot wrong, twisting it, my red shoe falling off.

"Fuck this," I mumble under my breath. As I limp to my car, leaving the shoe behind, I realize this is the perfect time to call things off. The divorce just went through, and our summer is done.

I still have Hitched. I still have Tate and Vi and everything I'm building in my life. I don't need Sebastian.

As I pull my note out of the box and stuff the box into Sebastian's mailbox, my phone rings.

It must be the client who just booked. I answer with a voice I hope doesn't betray my emotion.

"Hello, is this Ms. Michaels?"

"Yes."

"This is David Melton's assistant. I'm calling as a courtesy to let you know that while we appreciate your creative ideas for the bachelor party, we've decided to go with a different company for that evening. Mr. Melton thanks you again for your enthusiasm and wishes you the best."

I hang up, my heart shriveling into something dark and sad as I realize that my love life and my plans for my business have both fallen apart on the very same night.

Fuck. This. Shit.

THIRTY TWO
Moving on

"What happened?" asks Tate, looking me over like I caught some ugly disease.

I know I look like shit. My mascara's running, and my face must be red. "It's over," I say as I rush to the bathroom to get cleaned up.

Tate follows me, anger in his voice. "What'd he do, sis?"

"Nothing. The divorce went through. Now, we can both get back to normal—"

"Don't give me that shit, Kacie. What the fuck happened?"

I run my hands under cool water, then splash it on my face. The memory of Sebastian and Celene still burns. "I realized I can't be in a serious relationship and run Hitched, okay?" *And Sebastian needs someone else.* Then I remember with a sinking heart that's not all that happened tonight, and the rest involves Tate and his life too. "Speaking of Hitched, you were right. The basket was a lame idea, and it didn't work. We lost the Melton party. They picked someone else. Maybe if I hadn't been with Sebastian, hadn't been distracted, I wouldn't have fucked it up. I would have figured out a way to get that client and make our careers."

"First, don't worry about Hitched. The business is fine. We don't need a big client to do well. Second, I'm calling Vi," says Tate. "You need her."

Before I can object, he disappears down the hallway. I jump into the shower. Thoughts of Sebastian, his fingers on my skin, his lips on my mouth, fill my mind, but I push them away. Fuck that man. I have to get over him if I'm ever to enjoy life again. Seeking distraction, I get out of the shower, throw on a soft large shirt, and dig into a bowl of chocolate chip ice cream. Tate turns on *The Princess Bride*, one of those movies we could watch forever, and we sit together on the couch, my head resting on his shoulder. A few minutes later, Vi arrives, holding a white bag.

"I've brought the break up cure," she says, pulling out a giant bottle of vodka.

"I think we might need more than that," says Tate.

Vi nods knowingly and pulls out a second bottle.

"Are you trying to kill me?" I ask.

"Girl, you're killing yourself," says Vi, pouring us shots, and by shots I mean full fucking cups. She hands me one. "Dr. Sexy isn't worth it."

You're wrong, says a part of me. The part that still thinks Sebastian is the greatest man in the world, and I'm stupid for leaving him. But I can't be with someone who's so ready to marry me, or so ready to be with someone else. I don't even know which it is, but I'm not ready to commit, and he deserves someone who is.

"Keep the drinks coming," I tell Vi.

She smirks and cuddles up next to me. By the end of the film, when the grandfather says, "As you wish," we're all teary eyed and drunk as fuck. "You're not supposed to be sad," I say, my words slurring. "You're never sad."

Vi is crying so hard she gasps. "I broke up with Chad."

Tate and I speak in unison. "What?"

"I left him," she says in between sobs. "Oh shit. I'm sorry. I'm supposed to be cheering you up."

"Don't apologize. And don't fucking lose it on me." I grab her drink and refill it, channeling Vi when I say, "Mr. Musician isn't worth it."

She chuckles, wiping her eyes and taking the drink.

Tate sighs. "Are there no fucking gentlemen left?"

"That's the problem," says Vi. "He was *too* gentle."

Yeah. That could be a problem. But not with Sebastian—

I stop thinking and slap myself. Hard. On the face.

"What the fuck are you doing?" asks Tate.

"I'm cutting out the bullshit. We need to go out. Now. And do something crazy." I grab their arms and pull them off the couch. "Let's go to a club." I make it two steps.

And collapse onto my comfy chair. "Fuck."

"Maybe tomorrow, sis." Tate and Vi fall back on the couch, Tate restarts *The Princess Bride*, and we pass out in a few minutes.

...

A knock on the door wakes me. My mouth tastes like dirt, and my head is pounding, but I force myself to stand up. Vi and Tate are still asleep on the couch, despite the loud banging. Lucky bastards. I open the door.

And see Sebastian.

Shit. My drunk brain forgot about him. If it hadn't, I wouldn't have opened the door for days.

He steps forward, reaching for me. "I got your package. I know you think you're not ready—"

"I'm not." I back away, because I need my resolve to end this, and the touch of his fingers will steal it. I don't even bring up Celene. I tell myself it doesn't matter, that this had to happen even if she hadn't been there yesterday. I'm not curious about why she was there. At least, these are the lies I feed myself. It almost works.

"Let me finish. I need you, Kacie. No matter what, I need you in my life. I would never ask you to give up your job. But I need to ask you to stay with me."

"I tried," I say, wanting to run into his arms. "But I can't be with you. Not now."

"Then I'll wait for you."

"Don't waste your time. I'm not going to change my mind."

"Kacie, it wouldn't be a waste."

I almost break into tears at that. "You need to leave," I say, starting to close the door on him.

He holds the door open, stopping me. His eyes are sad. "If you reconsider, let me know."

At that moment, I know he won't get over me. So I do what I have to. "I met your one condition. I spent the summer with you, and now we're done. Don't come over here again. Don't text me again. Stop messing up my life."

His jaw tenses. "You don't mean that."

I don't. But I can't say it. I can't say anything. So I close the door on him and let the tears flow.

...

For the next week, I bury myself in work. Joey has a friend getting married for the second time, and the party needs to be something new, so we're all going horseback riding. *I will not think about Sebastian. I will not think about Sebastian.* This has become my mantra.

We receive a referral from Dan, and I wonder if this is Sebastian's way of meeting me again. But I doubt it. He hasn't texted me since we broke up. I wish he had, but it's a stupid wish because I'm the one who told him not to. See, these kind of annoying thoughts are the reason I stay focused on Hitched and working out. Tate and I run every day, and every day he asks me how I'm doing. I say "fine," hoping that if I say it enough, it will be true.

Vi is going through her own emotional turmoil. Ever since her breakup with Chad, she's taken on more clients but doesn't seem any happier.

"Is there any chance for you two?" I ask as we sip coffee at Starbucks one morning.

"He'd take me back," she says, picking the blueberries out of her blueberry muffin. "But I don't really love him, and I can't keep hurting him. It's more than just sex for him."

"I thought it was more for you, too."

"I wanted it to be more." She finishes the muffin and cleans her long manicured nails. "But some people just aren't right for each other, even if they're both amazing people."

"Like me and Sebastian," I say.

She grins. "I wasn't talking about you." I can tell she wants us to get back together. She doesn't really agree with the whole "not ready" thing. "True love doesn't happen every day" is her motto. Well, the motto she stole from *The Princess Bride*.

The bachelor party on Wednesday goes fine. It's only a hotel room with strippers, but the groom seems to enjoy it.

When the weekend arrives, Tate convinces us to go out. "I'm tired of seeing my ladies moping around," he says. "Like you said Kacie, we need to do something crazy. So we're hitting a club, and I want everyone to get laid tonight."

He's right. I should try to move on, so I put on my sexiest red dress and high heels—not my red ones because I'm still missing the one I lost at Sebastian's—and we meet up with Vi at the club. "Three shots of vodka," I tell the bartender, knowing I'll have to be very drunk to even have a chance at hooking up. Sebastian is too often on my mind. I need to drown him out.

"He's cute." Vi points at a guy dancing alone, his arms thick, his blonde hair short and curly. He doesn't even compare to Sebastian.

"I hate him," I say.

Vi frowns. "Well if you feel that strongly, there is that guy over—"

"Not him." I down another shot. "Sebastian. I hate Sebastian." *Because he's too fucking perfect and has ruined all other men for me.*

"Then give Curls a chance," says Vi.

"Curls?" We both laugh, and I check out the guy on the dance floor again. "You can have him."

"I most certainly will." She throws back her last shot, grabs her purse, and saunters across the dance floor. Curls notices her right away, and they start dancing.

Tate puts a hand on my shoulder. "If you can't get your mind off Sebastian, then what help are you going to be with Hitched?"

I brush his hand off. "I've worked all week."

"You've *tried* to work all week. I'd rather have the happy Kacie who fantasizes about her next date and keeps sexting her boyfriend, her passion bleeding into her career, then the one with a broken heart who can't find the joy in anything."

I feel like cussing him out, but I can't, because he's right. "I pushed him away," I say. "Even if I wanted to change things, it's too late."

"I'm sure Sebastian disagrees."

"Maybe." *But I can't face him again.*

Tate stands up. "While you think about what I said, I'm going to go find a girl to fuck." He starts dancing with a blonde he'll probably never see after tonight, and I order another drink.

Vi is right.

True love doesn't happen everyday.

THIRTY THREE
Thoughts and Memories

I try to forget about him. I do everything I can to wipe the memory of his scent out of my mind. To erase the thoughts of how his hands felt on my body.

But my dreams betray me.

Night after night I wake, expecting him to be snuggled up against me, hogging the sheets, and every day I'm disappointed by the cold, empty betrayal of my lonely bed.

So I do what I've always done in the past. I throw myself into my work.

Fall has come, and the weddings and crazy bachelor parties have slowed down. We knew this would be the case. We planned for it. Still, I feel the pinch of it financially and am forced to cut down on my trips to Starbucks and nip my budding wine addiction in the bud. Probably for the best, that one.

With renewed determination to not be a pathetic lump of a human, I grab my car keys and a water bottle, along with a box of business cards. "Tate, I'm heading to the Strip to proselytize. Be back in a few hours."

He looks up from his computer. "That's a great idea. Want some company?"

"Nah, I got this. You work on those newspaper ads."

He salutes me. "Yes ma'am."

It may be fall, but it's still hot as hell during the day.

I park in one of the hotel lots and map my route. The mission is to hit up as many hotels as possible, letting the concierge know the awesome services that Hitched has to offer and to build personal relationships. This business is all about referrals, and no one does referrals like a concierge who likes you.

I also have a side mission that I didn't tell Tate about. I check my purse to make sure the letter I slaved over is still in there. Yup. I make it my first stop, heading to the Wynn to get this into the hands of David Melton himself.

Vi knows the concierge there. I don't ask how. And he's going to help me.

When I arrive and introduce myself, the mousy man smiles. "Mistress Vi speaks highly of you," the concierge says. "Come, let us do this thing."

I refrain from laughing as he sneaks me to the penthouse suite and knocks on the door of Melton's room. I'm not sure who I'm expecting to answer the door, but I'm actually shocked to see the man himself standing there, dressed in black silk pajamas, his dark hair messy, his handsome face different without all the stage makeup. I almost forget how to speak.

He looks like he just woke up, and I realize this is probably early for him. I quickly introduce myself and hand him the letter. "I know you've chosen someone else, but if that doesn't work out, please consider Hitched. I know we can make your night memorable."

I wait, breath held, as he looks at my letter. "Well, Ms. Michaels, you're certainly committed to your work. I admire that. I'll read this over, but as my assistant told you, we have already commissioned another company to plan the party."

"Yes, I understand. But I couldn't walk away without giving it one last try."

He smiles. "That will get you far in life. Have a good day."

He closes the door, and my bones turn to Jell-O. I thank the concierge and text Vi, thanking her for the connection, then continue my sales pitch down the Strip.

I've handed out a dozen cards when I stop in front of *the* hotel. The one I met Sebastian in. I take a deep breath and brace myself, then walk into the cool, air-conditioned lobby.

I expect everything to remind me of him, and it does. And I'm not emotionally prepared.

I bite my lip to keep from crying and walk faster toward the concierge. He's tall and wiry with a shock of red hair that looks like it's trying to escape his head. He smiles widely as I approach.

"Hi, I'm—"

Before I can introduce myself, he cuts me off. "Mrs. Donovan, yes! I remember you. You and your husband stayed here. It's so good to see you again. I love meeting happy couples after I've had the honor of witnessing their nuptials."

"You were at our wedding?"

He frowns for a moment, then smiles again. "Yes, of course. I helped arrange it and stayed as witness. But I understand it was an exciting evening, and there was much celebrating. It's no wonder certain memories have become a bit blurry."

I keep a smile frozen on my face and pretend I still know how to behave like a normal human being. "Yes—no, I mean, of course I remember you. Thank you so much for all of your help." The words are hard to say, like they're stuck in molasses, but I get them out and hope he doesn't notice how odd I'm behaving.

"It was my pleasure, of course. Oh! Before I forget..." He reaches under his desk and pulls out a manila envelope. "Sorry this took so long. I was going to mail these but since you're here..." He hands it to me.

"What is it?"

I open it up and pull out the contents.

"Pictures from your wedding night."

The rest of the conversation is a blur. I hand him a card, which he accepts enthusiastically, assuring me he will indeed recommend us to everyone he knows, and by the way, he also has friends at other hotels, and he'll make sure they too use Hitched for all their party needs. I thank him, assure him Sebastian and I are still happily married, and I leave.

I'm walking too fast. I know I am. But I can't breathe, and I can't stop, and I just have to get home before I am completely destroyed by what I'm holding.

Somehow I manage the drive home through a blur of tears, and I ignore Tate as I run up to my room, lock my door, blast music and collapse onto my bed.

Because apparently I'm sixteen again, but whatever.

Only then do I allow myself to finish looking at the glossy 5x7 photographs I didn't even know existed.

I expected to look like a drunken mess, since that's how I always pictured the night in my mind. But the reality of the pictures is much different.

I look...happy. So incredibly happy and free and full of life and joy and hope.

In every picture, Sebastian and I are together—smiling, laughing, kissing, loving.

And as I flip through them, the memories finally emerge, strong and unabbreviated. Every moment of that night crashes into me. I remember our talks, how even in one night this man "got me" in a way no one else ever had. I remember the long walk where we bared our souls. Where I cried over my own loneliness and fears, where he confessed his deepest regrets, where we shared every tidbit of our lives.

And I remember why I married him.

Because he made me feel whole. Not because I'm incomplete without him, but because with him, I can see myself reflected in his eyes, and I see how complete I really am. How complete I've always been.

THIRTY FOUR

Another Heart to Heart

The first call I make isn't to Sebastian. It's to his mom.

"Hi, Sylvia. It's Kacie."

Her voice sounds cheerful. Not suspicious and full of rage, as I'd feared. "Kacie, it's good to hear from you. How are you?"

I swallow the lump in my throat. "Um, I've been better. I was wondering if you had time to talk. I need some advice, and I didn't know who else to call."

"Of course, dear. Would you like to come to the house? We can have lunch and relax by the pool?"

"Yes, that sounds great. Would...today work?"

I can hear the smile in her voice. "Sure, why don't you just head out now? By the time you get here, I'll have everything ready."

The drive feels far too long, but I finally arrive and am once again blown away by the majesty of their home. Sylvia greets me at the door and invites me in. "We've got the house to ourselves for a few hours. So no need to worry about interruptions."

"Thank you for agreeing to meet with me. I'm sure you're very busy."

I help her bring our plates and glasses out to the backyard, and we sit by the pool. She's made a beautiful chicken salad with hummus and veggies on the side and fresh orange juice. Everything tastes delicious, and we eat in silence for a few minutes before I speak. "Did Sebastian tell you everything about how we met?"

She smiles kindly. "I know you got married in Las Vegas the night you met."

Well, this will go easier then. "Yeah. I couldn't remember all of that night for a long time. You must think I'm awful."

"Not at all. I think you two are young, and it was impulsive, but hardly the worst thing in the world."

"And we agreed to date over the summer, while our annulment went through. But the day I got the papers and went to show him, he was with his ex."

She nods but doesn't say anything.

"I know I overreacted. I didn't actually see them doing anything. I don't think he cheated on me—though I haven't actually asked him, but seeing them together made me question everything about our relationship. Whether we were really meant to be together. Whether Celene was a better fit for him, because of their careers and lifestyles. And I got scared. Really scared."

I take a sip of the orange juice before continuing. "I broke his heart. I know I did. And I broke mine too."

"And now?" she asks.

"Now, I don't know. I'm still scared. I'm still not sure. How do you know when you've met the right person? How do you know it will work out forever?"

"You never really know it will work out. That's a choice you both have to make each day. As to how you know if you've met the right person, I think that's something for which you have to look inward for an answer. But I don't think you'd be here now if you didn't already know the answer."

I take out the envelope of pictures in my purse and hand them to her. "I got these recently, from the night of our shotgun wedding. When I saw them, I remembered everything."

She flips through the photos, her face unreadable. When she finishes, she hands them back to me. "You two look very happy. A bit drunk, but very happy. I've never seen my son like that, but I'd like to."

"Part of me knows I made a huge mistake breaking up with Sebastian, but the other part of me is still scared I'll lose myself in him. Lose my career, lose everything I've worked so hard for. I'm not like the people from his work, the other doctors. I'm sure they look down on my business and what I do for a living. But it matters to me."

"Does Sebastian look down on it?" she asks.

"No."

"Has he said he'd want you to quit if you stayed with him?"

"No."

"Then what does it matter what anyone else says? The most important thing in any marriage is that you both decide together what kind of life you want, and then you work hard to make that happen no matter what the outside world thinks about your arrangement. I know there are people my husband works with who think he's less of a man because his wife makes more money. And people I've worked with in the past who think I'm a ball-busting bitch because of my success or business acumen. We discussed these things early on and agreed it didn't matter. We'd never let it bother us or come between us. And we certainly wouldn't let it interfere with our happiness."

"And that worked?" I ask. "It really never bothered either of you?"

She shrugs her shoulders. "We had our days. But generally, no, it never did bother us. Because we chose each other and our life over the thoughts of others. I have always been of the philosophy that what other people think of you isn't your business. It's theirs. So the question you need to ask yourself is, does being with Sebastian make you happier than being without him? And has he ever actually gotten in the way of your career?"

I know the answers to both of those questions. Which leaves me left with one question of my own. "How do I get him back?"

THIRTY FIVE
Racing with the Stars

After talking with Sylvia and looking at our pictures so many times I have them all burned into the backs of my eyelids, I want nothing more than to show up at Sebastian's door and beg forgiveness for breaking up with him in the way I did. But I still can't decide the best way to win him back. I need something big. Magical. Unforgettable.

It's in the middle of all this teenage-like angst that I get the call.

"Hello?"

"Ms. Michaels?" The voice is male. Deep. Vaguely familiar though I can't place it. "This is David Melton. You had contacted me about my bachelor party?"

O.M.G. I can't breathe. I try to breathe. I need to talk. To say something. Anything. "Yes?"

"I want to apologize. My assistant chose a different company and called you to let you know, but we have a problem. The company he chose has botched things up. I was impressed with you when we met briefly the other day. So my question is, can you take over at the last minute and make some magic? Are you still up for the challenge?"

I look at my calendar. His bachelor party is supposed to be tomorrow night. I'm screaming in my head, but I remain outwardly calm. "Are you asking me to plan your party by tomorrow night?"

He clears his throat. "Yes, that's exactly what I'm asking. There will be a generous bonus in it for you if you can make it happen. Your ideas were excellent. I would consider this a personal favor if you could make something epic happen."

"I can't promise it will have all of the elements I originally promised, but yes, I can give you a night you won't forget."

"Excellent. My assistant will be in touch and can get you any other details you need. I look forward to seeing you again tomorrow night. Thank you."

My heart is racing as I call Tate and Vi with the good—and insane—news. "We got it. Get home now! We need all hands on deck to pull this off."

Thoughts of Sebastian still flit around in my mind, but I'm in full-on panic mode, making calls to secure the cars, the helicopter, the roof of the Wynn Hotel, the dancers, the music, the food, the alcohol, the lighting…everything needed to make this night "epic."

Tate is on the phone with vendors. Vi is working with the dancers to come up with something original. We're all busting our asses to make this work.

...

The night of the party, I'm a nervous wreck.

Every moment not spent in planning was spent watching David's shows, getting a sense of his style. The evening needs to have a flare of the dramatic. He's a bit goth, a bit punk, all wrapped up in the world's sexiest magician, who will now be off the market for good.

His wife is a popular actress who's widely recognized. I'm bummed I won't get to meet her tonight.

We arrive at the Wynn well before anyone else and spend hours setting up. When David and his friends arrive, he's all smiles. "Thank you again. You're life savers."

I introduce him to Tate and Vi, and caterers bring out food and non-alcoholic drinks. "Don't get too comfortable. The helicopter will be here soon to take you to your first adventure. Then we'll come back for drinks, dancing and more fun."

On cue, the helicopter arrives and lands on the helipad.

"I can't believe you managed this on such short notice," David says, pulling himself into the helicopter.

It takes a few trips, but we eventually get everyone to the race tracks where sleek cars in reds, yellows, blues and blacks wait to be driven.

The guys are given instructions and assigned to their cars, which they drive with gleeful speed around the racetracks.

After they finish a few laps, all of them laughing and slapping each other's backs, I pull David aside. "I have one other surprise for you."

I nod my head to Tate who ducks away and comes back with someone else. As they get closer, David raises his hands to his face in shock. "No, you didn't. Fuck! Is that really Michael Schwartz?"

"It is!" It took some doing, but it turns out Schwartz is just as big of a fan of David as David is of him and was thrilled to meet the magician. I lean over to David. "I promised him VIP tickets to your next show. I hope that can be arranged?"

He hugs me with exuberance. "Of course. You can have anything. I'm in your debt forever." He kisses my forehead then reaches his hand out to the famous racecar driver. "It's a pleasure to meet you."

"Same to you," Michael says with a smile. "Care to go a few laps with me?"

I'm worried David's going to pass out from excitement, but they do a few laps at speeds that make me nauseous, and Schwartz flies back with us for the rest of the party.

Tate high fives me as we climb into the helicopter after them. "Good job, sis. You made the impossible happen."

Back at the party, we serve the drinks (this time with alcohol) and more food as the dancers begin their intro dances. We worked hard to create a new routine with them that included a bit of magic tricks, and some escapes from handcuffs on the pole.

David seems to enjoy himself during the bulk of the show and claps the loudest when the dancers do their handcuff trick.

As the men get lap dances or refills on their drinks, David comes over to me. "This is incredible. You've made this night more spectacular than anything I could have imagined."

"I'm so glad. It's been my dream to do a party like this, so thanks for taking a chance on our little company."

"Not little for long. I just called Richard Morgan and told him he has to use you for his bachelor party in two months."

My mouth falls open. "*The* Richard Morgan. Movie star Richard Morgan? Most eligible bachelor for like—ever—until recently, Richard Morgan?"

David laughs. "The one and only. He's on board. Expect a call from his assistant sometime next week. Kacie, Hitched is about to blow up. I hope you're ready for some serious expansion."

This time I hug him and kiss his cheek. "Thank you. Thank you so much!"

He throws a friendly arm over my shoulder as we watch the dancers do their next routine. "You're a pretty incredible woman, Kacie. What's your story? You married? In love? Kids?"

My face drops, and I surprise myself by telling him the raw truth, not the professional whitewashed answer I'd normally fall back on. "In love? Yes. Married? Not entirely. It's complicated, but the short story is, I had the perfect man, and I gave him up out of fear. Now I'm trying to figure out a way to tell him how I feel and get him back."

David smiles the smile of someone who has an idea that's either very brilliant or very dangerous. "I might be able to help with that."

THIRTY SIX
The Magic Trick

I've been waiting two weeks for tonight. Two long, painful, busy, emotionally loopy weeks. Two weeks during which time our business has literally exploded. We're now in the process of hiring a whole new team to handle all the celebrity parties, thanks to David. Two weeks I had to resist my urge to knock on Sebastian's door.

Instead, I talked his mom into helping me with the plan David and I created.

Lure him to David's show under the guise that his mom got two amazing tickets and wouldn't he please be her date? Of course he said yes. Not only is he a huge fan, but he would do it just to spend time with her.

The plan worked. They are both in the audience right now.

I am backstage and blind folded. David doesn't want his secrets revealed, and I'm part of one of his big magic tricks. So I'm waiting. Listening to the show, to the crowd's applause, to the performance David is so skilled at giving. I wait in the dark, hoping—praying—that I'm not making the biggest mistake of my life. Hoping that I don't make

Hitched

a fool out of myself and get my heart broken to pieces in front of hundreds of people. Hoping I don't ruin David's show.

Someone touches my arm. "Your part's almost here. You doing okay?"

I nod, sitting in a chair, my formal red gown tight around my chest. Is that why it's hard to breathe? Or is it just nerves? I inhale. And wait.

And then I hear him pick Sebastian from the crowd. "Sir, come up on stage and introduce yourself."

Sebastian's voice makes me melt. "I'm Sebastian Donovan."

"And what do you do for a living?"

"I'm a—"

"Wait, let me guess—you work with kids…you're a doctor. A pediatric heart surgeon!"

I can hear the shock in Sebastian's voice. "Yes, actually. That's incredible."

"Have we ever met before, Sebastian?"

"No."

"Okay good. Now, I'm going to ask you to help me with my next bit of magic. Is that okay?"

"Sure."

"Great. Now see that frame right there with the picture of the beautiful woman in shadows? Can you tell who she is?"

"No."

"Okay, great. Now I want you to imagine the love of your life. The one who got away. The girl you wish were here right now so you could tell her how much you love her. Are you picturing her in your mind now?"

215

"Yes." Sebastian's voice sounds different, and I wonder what he's thinking.

"Stare at the painting and keep imagining her. Picture every detail of her, from the color of her hair to her eyes, to the way she smiles. Are you picturing it all?"

"Yes. I am."

"Great, now watch the painting closely."

The crowd gasps at something, and I can imagine it's the shadows parting to reveal a painting of me, but I can't see it. I can hear Sebastian though, when he inhales sharply. "How...how is this possible?"

"What's her name? The girl in the picture?"

"Kacie. Kacie Michaels."

My heart feels like a weight has been lifted from it. I've been living under this dreadful fear that he wouldn't picture me. Wouldn't say my name. That he'd pick Celene. And it would crush me. But he chose me. He picked me. I have to resist running out there right now and into his arms, but the magic trick isn't done yet.

"How would you like to see Kacie again? To hold her in your arms?"

His voice sounds sad. "I don't think that's possible, no matter how much magic you have." My heart breaks.

"Let's just see what we can do."

This is the part I'm blindfolded for. This is the part I have no idea how they manage. Because right now as someone moves me around by the hand, right now the crowd, and Sebastian, are seeing the painting literally come to life. The painting is turning into me right in front of their eyes, and somehow, when my blindfold is pulled off, I turn into a swirl of smoke and am standing on stage, facing Sebastian Donovan.

"Kacie?"

I step forward, my hands outstretched. "It's me. I'm here to say...I'm sorry. About everything. I love you. I've always loved you. And I don't want to live another day without you in my life."

The crowd "Awwws," David takes a bow, and we are ushered back stage.

I'm still waiting for Sebastian to reply, to say something, anything.

"Kacie..." He reaches for my hands, and when our skin touches, I feel warm and hopeful. A tear runs down my cheek.

"Oh Sebastian. I screwed up. I let my fear get in the way of the best thing that's ever happened to me. I'm so sorry. Please forgive me. Please tell me it's not too late."

He leans in, his hand reaching for my face, and he gently caresses my skin and kisses me deeply. His taste, his touch...it's everything I've been dreaming about. Everything I've wanted and needed for so long. I am home. With him, I am home.

"It's not too late," he says. "But I have one condition."

There's a twinkle in his eye, and a grin on his face.

"What's that?" I ask.

"Ninety days. You have ninety days to prove you really want to be with me. It's your turn, Ms. Michaels. Think you're up for the challenge?"

"I don't think you'll last ninety days," I say, smiling, and I kiss him again.

THIRTY SEVEN

Propositions

The kiss turns into something more, and we are scrambling to find an unused dressing room before our desire rips us apart.

We're already tearing at each other's clothes. I need him badly. I've needed him for so long, it's an actual pain in my body.

We find a room, more a costume closet than a changing room, but we aren't picky.

Sebastian closes the door behind us and locks it. I cough as a bit of dust shakes loose. "I think this is where the costumes come to die," I say.

He laughs and pulls me into his arms. "How did you manage all this?"

I look up into his handsome face, a face I thought I'd never see again, at least not like this. "Magic," I say. "Real magic."

He kisses me again, and our clothes magically fall off, joining the carcasses of costumes as our bodies find each other.

The sex is fast, hard, full of unfilled need left too long. His cock rams into me deeply, tearing me in half. We're standing, pushed against a wall, my legs wrapped around his waist as he fucks me.

It's raw, this coupling, as we pull our need out of each other, as we give everything we are to each other. My nipples are hard and so very tender as they brush against his chest with each thrust of our hips. I pull at his hair, and he groans and sinks his teeth into my neck.

We leave our marks on each other, and when we come, it is explosive.

After, we are spent, but we can't stay in the Closet of Lost Costumes forever. As we search for our own clothes, I see a new star on his back, and my breath hitches in my throat.

I trace it with my finger. "When did you get this?"

He turns, his face hard. "The day after we broke up."

"Who is it for?"

"Remember the little girl, Shannon? She died the night you dropped off the papers."

Oh God. Oh God, no. "Celene. That's why she was at your house?"

His face falls. "You saw that? Is that why? Oh my God. I'm such a fool. Yes, that's why she came over—to tell me. Shannon was her patient too. We try to keep it professional, to not care too much. You have to do that, to do your job well. But some of them just reach inside—they get to you. Shannon was like that, for both Celene and me. It was too much like losing Hope all over again. I don't love Celene, but I could offer her the small comfort of friendship that night. Nothing happened, Kacie. I hope you know that."

Tears run down my face. "I know that. And I'm sorry. I shouldn't have run. Shouldn't have hid behind my own fears. I've missed you every moment since that night."

He kisses me. "You'll never have to miss me again." Then he grins. "Assuming your ninety day challenge is a succes."

...

He makes it sixty days. Sixty days during which we spend nearly every moment together when we aren't working. Sixty days of learning more and more about each other, spending time with his family, going to events and art exhibits, playing chess, reading books, swimming, hiking, having barbecues with Tate and Vi and whomever they are dating that week. Sixty days of falling more and more in love with each other.

And then I get the package.

It's the red shoe I left at his house the night I arrived with our annulment papers. In it is a note with instructions of where and when to meet him. I remember the place. All of my memories have returned, and I'm grateful for that.

Everything is ready when I arrive. There's champagne and strawberries and a little table set up with all of my favorite foods.

It feels like an eternity as I sit there in the quiet chapel alone, candles flickering around me.

When he walks through the door, I release the breath I don't realize I'm holding.

He looks as handsome as I remember, and all my love, my lust, my desire, my need, it all topples over me in waves, and I want to throw myself in his arms, but I wait, nerves sending butterflies through my stomach.

"I got your package," I say, holding up a foot to show him the red shoe he rescued.

"I'm glad. I know I said we had to wait ninety days, but Kacie, I'm done waiting for what I want most in the world."

My breath hitches. "And what's that?"

He kneels before me so that we're face to face. "You."

I'm trembling from the briefest touch of his fingers against my cheek. "I want you, Ms. Kacie Michaels. Always and forever, I want you."

A tear trickles down my cheek and over the spot his finger just brushed against. "I want you too. Always and forever."

When we kiss, it's magic. It's everything in my life, everything in the universe, falling into perfect place. It's our fates intertwining fully and completely, without fear, without hesitation, without distraction.

And when he pulls away, I'm about to protest, but he takes a small box out of his pocket and holds it out to me.

"I've been carrying this around with me since the night you left the papers at my house. I couldn't give up hope that someday you'd come back to me, but I needed to be sure that this is what you want too. These last few months have shown me that we're ready for the next step. Kacie Michaels, will you marry me? Again?"

He opens the box, and a beautiful white gold ring sparkles at me. The main diamond is large, at least two karats, circled by smaller diamonds, with even more diamonds running down the band. It's magnificent.

Now my tears are flowing as I nod. "Yes, yes I will! Nothing would make me happier."

When he pulls the ring out of the box, I notice something engraved on the inside, and I laugh when I read what it says. "Hitched 06/02, Married 4Ever __/__".

"The first date is the day we got married, right here. The second date is yet to be decided, but it will be the date you become mine forever."

THIRTY EIGHT
Happily Ever After

I'm dressed in silk and lace, in a gown so elegant I'm scared to breathe, let alone move. Clara runs around, making sure everything and everyone is in place. Vi stands with me—I'm too scared to sit—and mumbles the occasional reassurance every few moments like a pre-recorded program.

When the text comes, I'm almost too nervous to pick up my phone. What if I chip my French manicure? Vi rolls her eyes and picks up the phone for me. "God, Kacie, you're not made of porcelain. Relax!"

"I just don't want to do anything to fuck up this day."

"Stressing to the point of immobilization is the only thing threatening to fuck up this day." She scrolls through my texts. "Lover boy says he can't wait to see you. He's fantasizing about you. He...Oh my, he sent a cock shot. He *is* as huge as you said."

I grab the phone from her and check it myself, and she just laughs.

"Figured that would get you moving again," she says.

No cock shot. Which is good, since I definitely don't want Vi checking out my soon-to-be husband. And a little disappointing, because...well...sexy cock shot from soon-to-be husband would have been yummy.

Guess I'll have to make do with memories. And future plans.

My parents are here, and my sister, who is also a bridesmaid, is helping Clara with something. I think mostly Clara is helping keep Jessica out of my way, which I appreciate. I can't handle too many people right now.

The Donovans went all out in decorating their home for my special day, and I'm in awe of how it's turned out. We debated between an indoor or outdoor wedding, and opted for indoors so I could come down their winding wrought iron staircase, now tastefully decorated with reds and silvers, the colors of our wedding in honor of the holiday season.

We won't get snow, sadly, but I'll settle for Christmas decorations.

Clara and my sister come back in and close the door behind them. "It's almost time," Clara says. "Are you ready?"

I nod, the pearls around my head tapping my forehead as I do.

Tate barges in and grins broadly. "Sis, you look stunning. Just had to see you before you make your big entrance."

He kisses my cheek, whistles to the bridesmaids and then exits as fast as he entered.

I look at my maid of honor and bridesmaids, each lovely in their red gowns carrying white roses. I've got red roses with white baby's breath. The contrast is stunning.

And against everyone's advice, particularly my mother's, I'm of course wearing the red shoes that have been with us every step of the way.

I peek down at them and then let my dress fall to the floor as Vi straightens me out and gives the okay to follow them down the staircase.

The live music begins, and the groomsmen meet each of the women at the top of the stairs and walk them down. I wait until the cue, and then meet my dad at the top, where no one can yet see me. He looks at me, and his eyes gloss over. "My little girl. You're all grown up. You look beautiful sweetheart."

"Thank you."

I will not cry. I will not cry.

Despite using waterproof makeup, I'm not convinced I won't look like a raccoon by the end of the ceremony. The only hope for me is not to cry.

I will not cry.

As we walk down the stairs, slowly, deliberately, in pace with the music, I search through the crowd until I see Sebastian standing in the center under the arch of flowers next to the pastor and his groomsmen.

Sebastian made Tate his best man. I would have made him my best man and broken all tradition—as was our plan since we were children—but he loves Sebastian so much, and my husband-to-be needed some padding on his side, so we broke with our plans after all.

As my eyes lock with Sebastian's and I see the love on his face and the joy he feels in seeing me, my heart swells.

And I know, no matter what else may happen in our lives, I'm looking at my forever.

And this time, I won't forget a moment of it.

THIRTY NINE
Déjà Vu

Our bed is disheveled in a way that only all-night fucking can accomplish. Empty bottles of Don Pérignon litter the high-end hotel room I've woken up in.

"Seems we had a bit too much to drink last night," Sebastian says with a smirk.

I'm holding one red shoe as I stare at this naked man in front of me. Tall. Dark. Sexy as sin.

"I can't find my other shoe," I tell him.

He strides toward me, water still glistening on his body from his recent shower. "I'm sure I can help you look. Later."

He touches me so gently, sending shivers up my spine, and my body instinctively arches into him. Even after an evening marathon of sex, I can't get enough of this man.

"Aren't we going to be late for our flight?"

"We have time," he assures me, pulling me back toward the bed.

I drop the red shoe, no longer caring where its partner is.

Heat throbs in my belly as he slides my panties off with ease. "You look good enough to eat," he says.

My legs spread as I lean back against the pillows. His head dips between my legs, his tongue teasing my labia.

"I need more than that," I tell him, grabbing his hair and pushing him harder against my clit.

He slides a finger, then two, into my wet pussy and uses his tongue to torture me.

The pressure builds inside me and then crashes through me in waves. I ride them, holding on to his shoulders, digging my fingers into his skin as he makes me come harder. Faster. Deeper.

Without warning, he flips me over until my ass is in the air, and he shoves his cock into me deeply as my body convulses with another orgasm.

I grip the headboard, rocking my hips against his, taking him all the way into me. He slaps my ass hard, and the shock of it intensifies my pleasure.

"Oh God, Sebastian. More. Fuck me harder."

He does.

So hard.

So deep.

So fast.

I soar with him inside of me, and then we collapse onto the bed, bodies intertwined together, satiated and happy.

...

I'm in the bathroom. Sebastian thinks I'm getting ready to leave on our honeymoon.

My hand shakes as I stare at the white stick, willing it to hurry up.

I don't know what I want it to say, whether I want one line or two. Whether I'm ready for the life-changing shock two lines would be.

I look down at my wedding ring and think about the man in the other room. My husband. And I realize that if it's two lines, I won't be alone. I'll have him every step of the way.

When the time is up, I look at the stick, and my heart tumbles around inside my chest.

I walk out of the bathroom, my hand still shaking as I hold the stick out to the man I married the night before. "Sebastian?"

He looks down at my hand, his face unreadable. He takes the stick from me and looks closely at it, then looks back up at me. "You're pregnant?"

I'm nervous. I don't know how he'll respond. Or if he's recovered from the loss of Hope. Or if he even wants children anymore.

But he smiles, tears filling his eyes, and all my fear is washed away. "We're having a baby?" he asks.

I nod. "Is...that okay?"

He wraps his arms around me and lifts me up, then kisses me. "Okay? It's better than okay. It's perfect. I love you so much, Kacie. Thank you. Thank you for filling my life with everything I've ever wanted, and so much more I didn't even know I could have."

He stole the words from my heart, and tears of joy roll down my cheeks as I press my face against his chest. "You've changed me, Sebastian," I tell him. "I used to be scared of that, but now I realize that it's a good thing, to be changed by love. I haven't lost anything at all, like I feared. Instead, I've gained everything."

He puts me down, wiping his eyes. "Remember the note I sent you?" he asks.

I remember. The note so sweet and tender I couldn't even share it with Tate. "Yes. It said, 'I remember our wedding, Kacie. I remember all of it, because it was the best day of my life.' That's it, right?"

He nods, grinning. "Well, I changed my mind. *This* is the best day of my life."

I laugh, shaking my head as I pull his lips to mine. "No, my love. The best days are yet to come."

THE END

Continue the story and find out what happens next to Kacie, Sebastian, Vi, and Tate, in *Whipped*—a *Red Shoe Memoir* focused on Vi, the Dominatrix, and Lachlan MacKenzie, the sexy Scotsman who changes everything. Look for it now at your favorite book retailer.

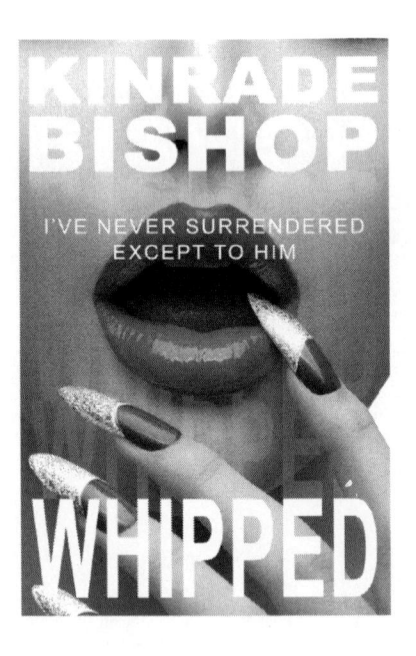

What happens in Vegas…might destroy you. Or remake you all together.

I make a living giving men and women their ultimate fantasies…as submissives of the mysterious Mistress Hawthorne. I've never surrendered to anyone. That's not the way it works. Or rather, not the way I operate. But when the gorgeous Lachlan MacKenzie shows up in my life, he throws everything out of balance.

Now I'm not even sure who I am anymore, and I'm questioning everything: my career as a Dominatrix, my next step, my role in the bedroom...What woman can turn away from a gorgeous Scotsman, especially when he sets her body on fire and her heart ablaze?

But I have to stop it...us. I can't keep going like this. Who am I if I surrender to him? Worse yet, who am I if I don't?

Whipped is a sexy, full-length, stand-alone romance in The Red Shoe Memoirs. These books can be read in any order.

CONTENT WARNING: This book contains sex, swearing...and did we mention sex? Lots of sex. And abs. And Scottish accents.

THE RED SHOE MEMOIRS
* Hitched
* Whipped

Read on for a special chapter one excerpt of Whipped

No Naughty Deed Goes Unpunished

This isn't my usual client.

Normally, they come to me. It's discreet and makes everyone's life easier. But for certain people, you make exceptions.

My 1984 black Fiat convertible rumbles across the bridge, heading for the famous Las Vegas Strip. Cerulean clouds flee as the molten sunset dominates the sky, and I lay on the gas a little harder. I'm in no hurry—I never allow myself to be late. But with the wind dancing through my hair, the thrill of speed digs a bit deeper into my soul.

I review my gear, ensuring nothing is left to chance. Leather crop, purchased several years ago from a tack shop. Restraints in the form of scarlet cotton rope—silk ties are for movies and books. Entirely too slippery and time consuming. The usual detritus: blindfolds, clamps, rubber whips that range from noisy to pain-inducing. Sultry music, though I also brought a selection of classical entries on my iPad.

A quick check in my rearview mirror assures me that the Mac Russian Red lipstick I've fallen in love with provides just enough contrast so as not to clash with my long red curls. I even donned my glasses for the occasion, as opposed to my contacts. You'd be surprised how many men love a girl in specs.

My suit—pinstripe, skirted—fits my curves like a glove. Beneath, a dark leather and crimson corset meets a matching G-string, finished off with garters and stockings. My best friend's red stilettos complete the ensemble—my normal wardrobe would never include such a mundane shoe. The things I do for clients...

As I near the turn, I take a calming breath. There's always a bit of nerves, right before an introductory scene. This client is new, as are his interests. I have a website with a photo gallery and specialties listed, so he should know what he's getting himself into. But still...

Topping—or playing the Dom—requires you to know your bottom, or submissive. You can't push too hard or too far, as you risk injuring not only your client, but also the relationship that is tenuous at the beginning. But at the same time, if you go too light, or God forbid, too slowly, you lose future profits and referrals.

A balancing act. That's the best way to describe it. Sometimes, I wish I could be a submissive. A friend who enjoys playing the slave once told me that she loves turning inward, focusing on her own interests and pleasures, while the Dom does all the work. God, I wish I could let someone else run the show. But that's not the way it works. Or rather, not the way *I* operate.

Traffic on the strip is always brutal this time of day, but I get a few lucky breaks. I pull into the Wynn's parking garage with plenty of time to spare. I go over my notes, replay his application video on my phone, and try to gauge his personality and true desires.

Creating—or recreating—someone's fantasies requires imagination and research, but it also relies on innate skills. For this client, I have a pretty good idea of what he wants.

Who am I kidding? I know *exactly* what he wants. Because in reality, all of my clients want the same thing.

To let go. To be in the moment. To escape life.

Sounds amazing, doesn't it? I envy them in so many ways.

I head towards the hotel, following the maze of sidewalks into the main lobby. The Wynn is my favorite hotel on the Strip. The lobby is a fantasy of flowers and design, with twinkling lights, huge not-quite-real foliage, and an understated yet still garish beauty that sets it apart from any of the other lavish venues.

I nod to the concierge on duty and grab an envelope from him. We're old acquaintances, and I still owe him a drink for a favor he called in for me last year.

The elevator doors snick shut behind me, and I slip between the crowded space, falling against the back wall and closing my eyes. For once, my outfit doesn't draw hushed comments, as besides the skirt that barely covers my ass, I'm pretty low-key in a city of gorgeous dancers and exotic delights of the flesh. Okay, maybe the shoes stick out a bit, too.

The elevator is empty by the time I reach the top public floor. Penthouse access requires a special pass card, and I extract mine from the envelope and slide it into the card reader. Then I wait while the elevator's silken glide ferries me to the top.

Stepping onto the lush carpet of the penthouse floor, I have two doors to choose from. I feel a bit like Alice in Wonderland, until I remember the room number the client texted me earlier today. With the Pixies' *Where Is My Mind?* forming an earworm in my brain, I knock.

A delicious man opens the door. Thick dark hair, lightly threaded with silver, strong jaw with an aquiline nose, sultry gray eyes that take in the length of me. He wears an exquisitely tailored suit that cuts across his impossibly broad shoulders in a mix of elegance and power. When he smiles, even my jaded heart quivers a bit.

"Mistress Hawthorne. A pleasure."

I level a gaze at him, knowing that my red curls and green eyes captivate my clients. "The pleasure will be mine, Charles. Naughty boys have to be punished."

...

As a professional Dominatrix, I follow three rules:

1. Never let them disobey you.
2. Never let them touch you.
3. Never have sex with them.

At least, I used to follow them...

...

Check out more of our books at ReadKK.com

ACKNOWLEDGEMENTS

First and forever, we thank each and every reader who buys our books, reads them voraciously and tells their friends about them. We <3 you.

We have an awesome marketing and publicity team that we wish we could send chocolate and wine to on a daily basis. Anne Chaconas (Mistress BAM) of Badass Marketing is our spirit animal, and she can read our mind in ways that are terrifyingly accurate. Ally Bishop of BAM, and editor extraordinaire of Upgrade Your Story, helps make all our books the best they can be and puts up with our terrifying schedules and general insanity. She also comes to our rescue with emergency Skype calls when we just. CANNOT. Anymore. You're the best!

A huge thanks to our beta team. Cindyk, Nicole, Gemma, Amanda, Beth, Michelle, Tracy, Patti and Amy—you ladies are awesomeness in a bottle. We love you hard!

A special thanks to fellow author Alexia Purdy for her help in researching Las Vegas and answering all our random questions about daily life in a city we've only visited as tourists.

Finally, a huge thanks to the KK Naughty Club and all the bloggers who have read, reviewed and helped promote this book during launch! We adore you all in all your naughtiness.

ABOUT KARPOV KINRADE

Karpov Kinrade is the pen name for the husband and wife writing duo of bestselling, award-winning authors Kimberly Kinrade and Dmytry Karpov.

Together, they write fantasy, paranormal, mystery, contemporary and romance novels and hook readers into new and exciting worlds with writing that blends side-splitting humor, heart-wrenching drama, spine-tingling twists and sigh-inducing happily ever afters.

Look for more from Karpov Kinrade in the Seduced Saga, the Forbidden Trilogy and more coming soon.

They live with three little girls who think they're ninja princesses with super powers and who are also showing a propensity for telling tall tales and using the written word to weave stories of wonder and magic.

Find them at KarpovKinrade.com

On Twitter

On Facebook

And subscribe to their newsletter for special deals and up-to-date notice of new launches.

...

If you enjoyed this book, consider supporting the author by leaving a review wherever you purchased this book. Thank you.

Printed in Great Britain
by Amazon.co.uk, Ltd.,
Marston Gate.